KT-132-844

ALSO BY

AMÉLIE NOTHOMB

Tokyo Fiancée
Hygiene and the Assassin
Life Form
Pétronille

STRIKE YOUR HEART

Amélie Nothomb

STRIKE YOUR HEART

Translated from the French
by Alison Anderson

Europa Editions
214 West 29th Street
New York, N.Y. 10001
www.europaeditions.com
info@europaeditions.com

This book is a work of fiction. Any references to historical events, real people, or real locales are used fictitiously.

First Publication 2018 by Europa Editions

Translation by Alison Anderson
Original title: *Frappe-toi le cœr*

Library of Congress Cataloging in Publication Data is available
ISBN 978-1-60945-485-2

Nothomb, Amélie
Strike Your Heart

Book design by Emanuele Ragnisco
www.mekkanografici.com

Cover photo: pxhere

Prepress by Grafica Punto Print – Rome

Printed in Italy at Arti Grafiche La Moderna - Rome

STRIKE YOUR HEART

Marie liked her name. It wasn't as ordinary as one might think; it gave her everything she wanted. When she told people her name was Marie, it had a certain effect. "Marie," people would echo, charmed.

The name alone was not enough to explain her success. She knew she was pretty. Tall, with a good figure, her face lit with a blond radiance: she did not leave people indifferent. In Paris she might have gone unnoticed, but she lived in a town that was far enough away from the capital not to be considered a suburb. She had always lived there, and everyone knew her.

Marie was nineteen, and her time had come. She could sense that an extraordinary destiny awaited her. She was studying to be a secretary, which did not sound like much—but you had to study something. The year was 1971. Wherever you went, you heard: "Make way for the young."

She went to parties in town with people her age. When you knew people, there was a party almost every night, and Marie didn't miss a single one. After a quiet childhood and a boring adolescence, life was beginning. "From now on, I'm the one who matters, at last it's my story, it's not my parents', or my sister's." Her older sister had married a nice young man the previous summer and was already a mother. Marie congratulated her and thought, "The fun's over, old girl!"

It was a heady feeling, attracting people's gazes, making the other girls jealous, dancing until dawn, going home at daybreak, showing up late for class. "Marie, you've been out on the town again, haven't you?" asked the teacher, with mock severity every time. The ugly ducklings—unfailingly punctual at school—shot her looks full of rage. Marie sparkled, her laughter luminous.

If anyone had told her that belonging to the gilded youth of a provincial town augured nothing out of the ordinary for her, she would not have believed it. She wasn't planning anything, per se, she just knew that it would be tremendous. When she woke up in the morning, she could feel a powerful summons in her heart, and she let herself be borne along by her enthusiasm. The new day promised events, their nature as yet unknown. She cherished this impression of imminence.

When the girls in class spoke about their future Marie would laugh to herself: marriage, children, a house—how could she ever be content with that? How foolish to give words to one's hopes, and such petty words to boot? Marie did not name her anticipation; she savored the infinity of it.

At parties she liked it when the boys paid attention to no one but her. She, meanwhile, was careful not to show a preference for any one of them—let them all turn pale with fear they might not be chosen. Such a delight to have them all buzzing around her, coveting her, yet never gathering the nectar!

There was an even more powerful joy: arousing jealousy in others. When Marie saw the girls looking at her with such painful envy, her mouth went dry with pleasure. Greater still than this sensual delight was what those bitter gazes indicated: the story being told now was *her* story, her narrative, while the other girls were long-suffering extras, nothing more, invited to the feast to dine on the crumbs, destined for a tragic death from a stray bullet—in other words, from a burning sensation that was not meant for them.

Fate was concerned with Marie alone, and it was this exclusion of third parties that brought her such supreme, smug satisfaction. If anyone had tried to explain to her that the other side of jealousy was jealousy itself, or amounted to as much, and that there was no uglier sentiment, she would have given a shrug. As long as she was dancing, the center of attention, with a pretty little smile she could bluff her way.

The most handsome boy in town was called Olivier. Slender, with dark, Mediterranean looks, he was the pharmacist's son and would be following in his father's footsteps. He was kind, funny, and helpful, and liked by all, boys and girls alike. Marie did not fail to notice this last detail. All she had to do was show up, and bingo: Olivier fell madly in love with her. Marie relished the fact that it was so obvious. Now when the girls looked at her their painful envy turned to hatred, and she thrilled to the pleasure of their gaze.

Olivier misjudged the nature of her trembling, and believed himself loved. Overwhelmed, he dared to kiss her. Marie did not turn her face, but merely gave a sidelong glance to verify the abhorrence in which she was held. The kiss, for her, coincided with the sovereign triumph of her demon, and she moaned.

What followed thereafter obeyed a mechanism that was

a hundred thousand years old. Marie, who had been afraid it might hurt, was astonished to feel so little, except at the moment when everyone had seen them go off together. For the length of one night she loved incarnating woman's last best hope.

Hopelessly happy, Olivier did not hide his love. Now that she was a prima donna, Marie was radiant. "What a lovely couple! How well suited they are!" people said. She was so happy that she believed she was in love. Her parents' smiles enchanted her less than the ugly moue she saw on the lips of her peers. What fun, to be the star of this hit film!

Six weeks later she was singing another tune. She ran to the doctor, who confirmed what she had been dreading. Horrified, she shared the news with Olivier, who immediately put his arm around her.

"My darling, that's wonderful! Marry me!"

She burst into tears.

"Don't you want to?"

"Yes," she said, through her tears. "But I wanted things to be different."

"What does this change?" he replied, joyfully embracing her. "When two people are as in love as we are, children come very quickly, anyway. Why wait?"

"I would have preferred no one suspect anything."

He took this for modesty, and found it very touching: "They won't suspect a thing. Every single one of them has seen that we are madly in love. We'll get married two weeks from now. You'll still have the waistline of a young girl."

She fell silent, having run out of arguments. She worked out that fifteen days would not be enough to prepare the spectacular celebration she had been yearning for.

Olivier presented their parents with the fait accompli. He did not hide the reason for their urgency, which filled both mothers and fathers with enthusiasm:

"You didn't waste any time, kids! This is great, there's nothing like being young for having a baby."

"Sheesh," thought Marie, who put on a show of pride, in the hopes they would believe in her happiness.

The wedding was as perfect as any nuptials could be, given the haste. Olivier was exultant.

"Thank you, my darling. I've always hated those banquets that go on for hours and where you invite all these uncles you've never met. Thanks to you we are having a true love wedding, with a simple dinner and an evening spent with our closest family and friends," he said, as he danced with her.

The photographs showed a young man beside himself with joy, and a young woman with a forced smile.

Those who attended the ceremony were genuinely fond of the young married couple. No matter how closely Marie scrutinized their faces, she could not find a single expression of envy of the kind that might have convinced her that this was the most beautiful day of her life. She would have preferred to have had an enormous do with lots of jealous onlookers, malicious friends of friends, and neglected eyesores ogling a different wedding dress—not the one she was wearing, a simple affair that her own mother had worn.

"Can you imagine, at your age I was every bit as thin as you!" Marie's mother had cried on discovering that the post-war design suited her daughter so well.

Marie thought her remark was despicable.

The young couple moved into a pretty town house not far from the pharmacy. The bride would have loved to choose her furniture, but already by the second month of pregnancy she was overwhelmed by crushing fatigue. The doctor assured her that this was quite usual, particularly with first pregnancies. What was less normal was that her exhaustion lasted the full nine months.

She awoke only to eat, because she was constantly famished.

"I've stopped going to class, it's a pity," she said to her husband between two mouthfuls.

"In any case, you're far too intelligent to be a secretary," he replied.

She remained puzzled. She had never planned on being a secretary. For her, whether she studied shorthand or agronomy it was all the same. And besides, what did Olivier mean by "intelligent?" She refused to go into it any further and went back to bed.

There was something vertiginous about being able to sleep whenever she wanted. She would lie down and feel the abyss of sleep open beneath her, she would surrender to the fall and did not even have the time to think about it before she instantly disappeared. If it weren't for her appetite, she would never have woken up.

In her tenth week she began to crave for eggs. She called Olivier when he was already at the pharmacy:

"Make me some soft-boiled eggs. Seven minutes, not a second more or less."

The young husband dropped everything to run home and boil the eggs. They couldn't be made ahead of time, because soft-boiled eggs will continue to cook until they are eaten. He peeled them delicately and took them on a tray to Marie in her bed. The young woman devoured them with terrifying delight, unless he'd been distracted and had cooked them for seven and a half minutes—in which case she would shove them away and say, "It's stifling"—or six and a half minutes—in which case she'd close her eyes and moan how disgusting they were.

"Don't hesitate to wake me up in the middle of the night if you want some," said Olivier.

An unnecessary injunction: she did not hesitate. After eating her eggs she went back to sleep. It didn't take a genius to diagnose a case of sleep escapism, even if none of those close to her understood this. On the rare occasions when Marie was not asleep and indulged in thought, she would conclude, "I'm pregnant, I'm nineteen years old, and my youth is already over."

Then the abyss of sleep opened again, and she was relieved to sink into it.

While she ate her eggs, Olivier gazed at her tenderly and sometimes asked her whether the baby was kicking. She said no. The baby was very discreet.

"I can't stop thinking about him," he said.

"Me, too."

She was lying. For nine months she did not have one thought for the baby. Which she was right to do, because if she had thought about it, she would have despised it. Some instinctive precaution wanted her to experience pregnancy as a long absence.

"Do you think it's a boy or a girl?" he asked, from time to time.

She shrugged. If he suggested a choice of name, she turned it down. He respected her decision. The truth was that when she tried to focus on the baby, it didn't last a second. The baby remained radically foreign to her.

The birth was like an abrupt and unpleasant return to reality. When she heard the newborn baby's wailing, she was stunned: thus, all this time, she had actually contained someone.

"It's a little girl, Madame," said the midwife.

Marie felt nothing, was neither disappointed nor pleased. She would have liked for someone to tell her what to feel. She was tired.

They placed the child on her belly. She looked at it, wondering what sort of reaction they expected from her. Just then Olivier was allowed to come in and join her. He displayed all the emotions she was supposed to feel. Overcome, he kissed his wife and congratulated her, then, with tears in his eyes, he took the baby in his arms and cried, "You are the loveliest little girl I've ever seen in my entire life!"

Marie's heart froze. Olivier showed her the infant's face.

"Darling, look at the masterpiece you have created!"

Marie summoned her courage to gaze at the creature. The baby was dark, with black hair half an inch long. She had none of the red rashes that are so common among newborns.

"She looks like you, as a girl," Marie said. "We should call her Olivia."

"No! She's as beautiful as a goddess. We'll call her Diane," decided the young father.

Marie ratified her husband's choice, but once again her heart froze. Olivier placed the baby in her arms. She looked at her child and thought, "It's not my story anymore. It's yours."

It was January 15, 1972. Marie was twenty years old.

The little family went home. In the morning, Olivier gave Diane her bottle then left for the pharmacy. When Marie found herself alone with her daughter, she felt uneasy, and was at pains to understand why. She tried to look at her as little as possible. Changing her was not a problem. It was the baby's face that bothered her. When it was time for her bottle, Marie looked away the entire time.

She had visits, particularly in the beginning. Friends came by to see Diane. Every time, they lavished her with exclamations: "She's so beautiful! Unbelievable, such a gorgeous baby!" Marie tried to hide the pain she felt. What hurt most was the way her parents fell head over heels for their granddaughter.

"You've managed to have a baby who's even lovelier than you are!" said the grandfather.

His wife noticed that their daughter pursed her lips. She refrained from complimenting her, but Marie could see the adoring gaze her mother bestowed on Diane, and it grieved her.

She waited impatiently for the visits to be over. When the guests were gone, she put the infant in her cradle where she could not see her. She lay down on the bed and gazed at the ceiling and thought, "It's over. I'm twenty years old and it's already over. How can youth be so short? My story lasted only six months." It went round and round in her head. If only she could fall asleep, the way she had when she was pregnant! She no longer had the leisure to disappear, she had to face reality—it was an expression she had read somewhere, and she didn't understand what it meant, other than that it must be somcthing unbearable.

But Diane was a good little baby. She only cried at birth. Otherwise, not a peep. She smiled at everyone who looked at her. "How lucky you are," people said to Marie.

When Olivier came home from work in the early evening, he found his wife and daughter in bed, silent, a few yards apart. Where the infant was concerned, this didn't worry him, it seemed normal.

"I'm tired," Marie invariably replied to his worried inquiries.

"Do you want me to hire a nanny?"

His wife refused, wary at the thought of a stranger in the house.

"Your mother doesn't work. We could ask her to look after Diane," Olivier suggested one day.

Marie got angry.

"Why don't you say it, you don't think I'm capable of looking after my own child."

In fact, she knew that was what her mother would think.

The young father went to pick up his daughter, and he melted: she smiled as she made chirping noises. Olivier came out with one declaration of love after the other: "My beauty, my treasure, my joy!" He covered her face with kisses and did not notice that Marie was turning extraordinarily pale. He gave Diane her bottle and put her back in her cradle.

"My darling, you're so pale!" he cried, when he noticed his wife.

"I'll never have the strength to make dinner," she murmured.

"Let me take you out to eat!"

"We can't go out," she replied, gesturing with her chin at the cradle.

"Would you like me to call the babysitter?"

"I'll take care of it."

She was always careful to call Madame Testin, who was fifty-five years old and wore trifocals. She had to restrain her laughter when Madame Testin spoke to her daughter at close range and she saw the little girl sweetly turn her face away from the woman's bad breath.

At the restaurant, Marie was lively and regained some of her striking arrogance. The waitresses' envious glances did her the most good. She had chosen a restaurant where the waitress had been in her class at the lycée, because the cruelty of the comparison was a comfort to her.

Alas, her gallant Olivier spoiled the evening, saying, repeatedly, his voice dripping with love, "My love, I will never be able to thank you enough for our daughter."

Marie lowered her gaze to hide her vexation. Her husband was moved by what he took for modesty.

In the long run he grew worried. Months went by and the young woman was still not her old self. The girl he had married possessed a lust for life, but where had it gone? He would question her, but her answers were often evasive.

"Would you like to work?" he asked her one day.

"Yes. But it's impossible, since I dropped my studies."

"You're far too intelligent to be a secretary anyway."

"You already said that. So I'm intelligent enough for what, then?"

"I could use an accountant at the pharmacy."

"What do I know about accounting?"

"You could learn. I'm sure you'd be very good."

"And the kid?"

"I'll see to it—I'll explain to your mother that you can't study accounting and look after a baby at the same time."

Olivier went to see his mother-in-law, but he told her something completely different: her daughter was in the throes of postpartum depression, and only the prospect of work gave her the will to live. He begged her to be so kind as to look after her granddaughter. He would come and pick Diane up every evening.

"I'd be only too happy to," said the grandmother.

Once her son-in-law had left, the old lady let out her joy: "God bless Olivier!"

"I wouldn't have thought Marie was the depressive type," said the grandfather.

"Depressive my foot! She is pathologically jealous of her daughter. That's what's poisoning her."

"Why would she be jealous of her own little girl?"

"As if she needs a reason! You and I brought up our daughters to respect what is fair. We never gave more to one than to the other. Brigitte is the eldest, she's not as pretty as her younger sister, she is the one who could have been jealous. But she never was, and Marie is. I thought her problem had worked itself out: she is now the most beautiful woman in town, and she has made a fine marriage. Well, no: I've seen it with my own eyes, she's jealous of her daughter."

"What does she have to be jealous about—a baby!"

"Well, she's a lovely baby and she attracts attention: that's enough."

"You think she mistreats her?"

"No. Marie isn't unkind or crazy. But she doesn't show her any tenderness. It can't be very nice for poor Diane."

"How can anyone fail to love such a little angel?"

The grandparents took their granddaughter in and lavished all the more affection on her, because they knew that she was suffering from a lack of it. The baby's daily life changed completely and utterly.

Before, there used to be two high points in Diane's existence: morning and evening. They corresponded to the moments when her father came and took her from her cradle and covered her with kisses, changed her diaper, and gave her a bottle, showering her all the while with words of love. The stretch from one shore to the other, over the course of a day or throughout the night, lasted an eternity: during a century of light or darkness, nothing happened. Sometimes, the indifferent goddess would pick her up to change or bottle-feed her. This woman belonged so entirely to a foreign species that she managed to touch her without touching her, to look at her without seeing her. Diane opened her eyes wide in the hopes that the goddess would notice her presence, and even ventured now and again to produce a gurgle—in vain. When the goddess put her back in her cradle, the torture of hope ceased at last. Then, at least, Diane knew for certain that there was nothing to expect until morning or evening, but they would both be so far away that it was better not to think about them. She filled the void with questions: why was the smell of the goddess so familiar? Or, better still: why was that exquisite odor so heart-wrenching?

Suddenly, her life was transformed. Her father would

carry her off in a Moses basket and place her in the arms of a person who was the same age as Madame Testin, but this woman smelled very sweet and Diane loved the tender sensation she aroused. With her, the void vanished. When she wasn't holding her close to her heart, she put her in the playpen: her own space, but where she could see her Mamie. Mamie was as active and noisy as the goddess was passive and silent. Mamie prepared the food while listening to the radio, and she often spoke to it. When Mamie was eating, she would put Diane in a high chair and always gave her a taste of whatever it was she had cooked: she didn't have to try it, but she had the right to, and sometimes it was delicious.

Above all, Mamie looked at her and spoke to her. With Mamie she didn't only exist in the morning and the evening. She existed non-stop, and this was thrilling. Sometimes Mamie even took her out on amazing adventures. Together they would go to the market to buy vegetables, choose fruit, explore the world. There were no limits to the power Mamie had to make the world an interesting place.

In the evening her father came to collect the Moses basket, and his effusive greetings were delightful. They would go back to the goddess, who still didn't look at her, but who was feeling better. While she gave her a last bottle and put her to bed, Diane could feel that big body bubbling with life.

Olivier was right: Marie was enthralled with accounting. She was taking an intensive course, and it revealed all her gifts: numbers, which bored her in the absolute, became fascinating the moment they represented money.

Money had the aspirational value that aroused envy in others: Marie discovered that she had more money than most people in town, and she was jubilant. She immediately grasped the principle: you mustn't show that you liked it. That way, you could enjoy it all the more.

Not only did Marie turn out to be an ideal accountant, she was also an astute businesswoman: at the pharmacy, she created a counter for beauty products, and became their standard-bearer. Customers asked her for the secret of her fresh complexion and radiant skin. She refrained from telling them she was twenty-one years old and, as if letting them in on a secret, showed them a beauty cream that came with a very high price.

Olivier was more in love than ever with his spouse, and before long she was pregnant again. This time, she did not seem to be indisposed. She did not change her routine, and she went on working as usual.

One night she had a nightmare that is quite common among women who are pregnant with their second child: she dreamt that her first child died. She woke up in a paroxysm of anxiety, and felt she must make sure it was only a dream. She rushed to the cradle and reached for her little girl. Diane emerged from sleep upon sensing a miracle. The goddess was holding her in her arms and saying, over and over, "You're alive, you're alive!" She was covering her with kisses. Diane opened her eyes wide to see what she could make out in the gloom: the face of the goddess was utterly transformed, resplendent with tenderness and relief. So she released herself into the incredible turmoil of that embrace. Her entire being was transfixed with the most intense pleasure. The goddess's smell permeated all her senses, Diane was bathing in a perfume of ineffable sweetness and she came to know the headiest intoxication on earth: love. The goddess must, therefore, be her mother, since she loved her.

"Sleep well, my baby," Marie said eventually, placing the child back in her cradle.

And she went back to bed.

Diane did not fall asleep. The revelation of love continued to flow through her. To be sure, in the arms of her father, or Mamie, or Papy, she had felt she was loved and that she loved. But what she had just experienced in her mother's arms was of an altogether different nature: this was magical. It was a force that raised her up, transfixed her, crushed her with happiness. It was something to do with her mother's smell, which bore her away on the most exquisite fragrance. It was something about her mother's voice, which, when she had spoken to her that night, was the most delicious music she had ever heard. All of which was rounded out by the softness of her mother's hair and skin, which had ultimately transformed her embrace into a long, silken caress.

It was very important not to fall asleep: for her this was the only way to be sure she hadn't been dreaming. Diane had noticed that when you were asleep you could experience strange things. It took a certain time for your consciousness to let the unreal nature of those things sink in. But now, she noticed, it was the opposite: the longer she stayed awake, the less she doubted the truth of what had happened.

So this was it, then, the meaning, the rationale of all life: you were there, you put up with so much strife, you made the effort to go on breathing, and accepted so much that was dull, so that you would know love. Diane wondered whether there were other sources, beyond the goddess, that could cause it. She didn't think so: how many times had she seen her father snuggle in her mother's arms with a strangely blissful expression on his face?

Another mystery occurred to her: when the goddess had embraced her, she had felt her mother's heartbeat inside her, and she had realized that her own heart was beating in that big chest—but she had also heard another heart deep inside her mother, lower down. Did it have something to do with the unusual roundness of her beloved's tummy? And why did this feeling evoke confused memories, a nostalgia for unworldly intimacy?

Diane managed to stay awake, awaiting the morning with burning impatience. When her father came to get her in her bed for the morning ritual, she turned her face toward her mother to see if the change was still there. Her mother did not look at her, or say anything to her: a day like any other. And Diane knew that her mother had forgotten what had happened during the night. Even if she did eventually remember, she would think it had been a dream.

The infant felt her heart contract with pain. But inside her, something strong and clear whispered: "But I do remember, I know it wasn't a dream, I know that the goddess is my mother and I know that she loves me the way I love her, and that this love exists."

One morning, for no particular reason, Marie, not Olivier, took the little girl to her parents. During the brief instant she was in her arms, Diane sought her beloved's sweetness and perfume again, but her mother did not notice. Marie's father opened the door, and he saw the child's imploring expression and his daughter's indifference. He squeezed his granddaughter close and cuddled her:

"Good morning my pumpkin, my little sweetheart . . ."

"It's so ridiculous, to speak to her like that," said the goddess frostily as she strode away.

Flabbergasted by her attitude, the grandfather understood that his wife had been right. He saw the intelligent gravity in Diane's eyes and he decided to explain something to her:

"Your mother isn't cruel, my treasure. She's just jealous. She always has been, that's the way it is, there's nothing you can do about it. Jealous, do you understand that?"

The two-year-old said yes.

"It'll be our secret."

Had she already heard the word "jealous?" Whatever the case, she had the feeling she knew what it implied. And she saw it as a good sign: it was jealousy that was preventing her mother from showing her love. She had seen it on the goddess's face so many times: when her father would exclaim, "Diane, my little darling," when people admired someone besides her, her mother's features would harden and a mixture of spite and anger attenuated her beauty. It would last for a short while, and during that time she seemed to have trouble breathing.

Mamie arrived with a sigh.

"I'm not sure that was the right thing to do, to tell her."

"I knew!" declared the child.

The grandparents looked at her, astonished.

When they got back home, her father took her by the hand and led her into a room she had never seen, with a new bed.

"This is your new room, sweetie. Your mommy is going to have a baby who will sleep in your cradle. So you'll have your own bed, like a big girl. But until the baby comes, you can stay with us."

"Can I start sleeping here now?" she asked.

"Would you like that? Yes, you can."

Diane was enchanted to have this place for herself, and she moved her toys in there. She heard her father say to her mother, "That's good, the little one isn't jealous of the baby."

She thought: so that's how it is, she could have been jealous, too. The problem wasn't exclusively the goddess's. This reassured her in her belief that it was nothing serious.

She also wondered about the new baby. Would her mother be jealous of it, that way she was jealous of her?

One day, while she was eating with her grandparents, the phone rang. Mamie let out a cry and said, "We're on our way," and hung up.

"You have little brother," she announced.

In the car Diane realized she hadn't even imagined the possibility that the baby might be a boy. Would that change anything?

Maman was holding a tiny creature in her arms and gazing at it tenderly. Papa greeted his daughter with a smile:

"Sweetheart, come and meet Nicolas."

"Nicolas!" exclaimed Mamie. "He looks just like Diane, only he's a boy."

"You're right," said Olivier. "He's the spitting image of his sister."

Was that what I looked like when I was born? wondered the little girl as she gazed at the baby. She thought he was lovely, and she loved him. But what struck her was that her mother clearly adored Nicolas. She's not jealous of him, thought Diane.

"He's magnificent," said Mamie.

Maman thanked her, radiant. For the moppet, this was a revelation: it seemed her mother could enjoy a compliment directed at one of her progeny after all.

She had the answer to her question: yes, this changed everything, the fact that the baby was a boy. Strangely enough, Diane did not feel hurt. She was glad there was an explanation, it reassured her. She had never lamented the fact she wasn't a boy: what good would that do? And anyway, she was not sure she would have liked it better, being a boy.

"Can I hold him in my arms?" she asked.

Marie sat her daughter next to her in the bed so that she could hold her brother safely. Diane experienced a moment of magic: nestled against her mother, she could feel the warm, wiggly little life she had been entrusted with. Henceforth there was a new, important person here on earth.

Diane determined to give the whole matter some deep thought.

The first topic for analysis was her mother's preference for boys. Papa was a man: quite a damning piece of evidence right there. And that wasn't all. She had noticed that the goddess didn't behave in the same manner when she was in male company. She stood up straighter, was both more energetic and gentler, and she said the most remarkable things.

The second element to examine was jealousy. Could she conclude that jealousy was only expressed toward women? It wasn't that simple. Maman had already had occasion to vent her rage against Papa, rebuking him for having looked at some woman or other. One day she told him that she wasn't as important at the pharmacy as he was. In short, jealousy was founded on an obsession with competitiveness, and it did not mean she was opposed solely to women. It was getting complicated. And it was all the more complex in that the supreme aim of jealousy consisted in being regarded with envy by men and by women: oddly enough, at that stage there was no more discrimination.

There was no possible conclusion to all these ruminations: at the very least, Maman was happy to have a son. Anything that contributed to maternal happiness was good for the happiness of the entire world.

This time, Marie was not the least bit depressed. Within three days she was on her feet. A week later she was back at work at the pharmacy, fulfilling her role as Nicolas's devoted mother all the while. She asserted that maternity leave would not have been good for her morale. When she went to pick up the children at Mamie's in the evening, she rushed over to the baby to kiss him.

At one point the grandmother took Marie aside and said:

"You have the right to prefer one child over the other, but don't make it so obvious. It's hard on the little girl."

"I doubt that! She doesn't notice a thing."

"Don't you believe it. She's very advanced for her age, she is astonishingly precocious."

"Honestly, when it comes to Diane, people always exaggerate," said Marie, with that pinched expression Mamie knew only too well.

She's still jealous, sighed the grandmother to herself.

But the little girl did not seem to suffer because of it. When Mamie saw her covering her little brother with kisses, she admired her: by the looks of it, Diane was not jealous of the infant.

For Marie, just being happy was never enough, she wanted to flaunt her happiness before those who seemed less fortunate. To this end, she drew closer to her older sister, and invited her and her family to lunch every Sunday. The way to hell is paved with good intentions; similarly, the meanest intention can be a source of sincere joy. Brigitte, who was a sweet, kind woman, was glad of this, and to her husband she said:

"Motherhood suits my sister. She's lost her stuck-up side, she's made an effort to get close again. I'm so pleased."

"You're absolutely right, darling. I hardly recognize her, she has blossomed, she's charming."

In the presence of Brigitte, Marie was radiant, and could not stop thinking, "She went and married a roofer and she has two ugly, stupid daughters: how she must envy me!" In truth, Brigitte, who loved her life, was glad her sister had done so well. Véronique and Nathalie adored Diane and Nicolas. Alain got on marvelously with Olivier. The Sunday lunches were pleasurable moments for everyone.

Diane revered her cousins, who were two years older than she was, and twins. She found them adorable, these two little girls who were identical, down to how they were plump and smiled all the time. And it was so kind of Aunt Brigitte to bring a box of chocolates every time the way she did.

One Sunday after coffee Brigitte offered a second piece of chocolate to her niece, who loved chocolate. Marie stopped her:

"Out of the question. It's fattening."

"Oh, honestly, Marie, your daughter is thin as a rail!" said Brigitte.

"And she has to stay that way," said Marie.

Diane shuddered when she heard her mother's voice. Her words were unpleasant enough, but the way she said them, so harshly, was far worse, and the meaning behind it was not lost on her: "I don't like for my daughter to enjoy herself." She saw that Aunt Brigitte had noticed, too, and was shocked. The little girl hated it when there were witnesses to her mother's severity, for while she could, deep down, find a calming explanation for herself, she could not share it with others, or initiate them into her personal cosmogony, which could be expressed thus: "The goddess loves me, it's just that she loves me in a strange way, she doesn't like to show she loves me because I'm a girl, and her love for me is a secret."

When her sister wasn't looking, Aunt Brigitte put her arm around her niece and whispered in her ear: "I have a chocolate in my hand, and I'm going to put it in yours."

"No, thank you, Auntie, I don't want any."

Her aunt did not insist, but gave the little girl a puzzled look.

When Brigitte and her family had left, Marie always made a few disparaging remarks: "The twins have put on weight, don't you think?" Or: "Have you seen the way Alain wolfs down his food: you'd think he doesn't get anything to eat at home!"

Olivier shrugged off these nasty comments, which for him were just a sign of the affection between the two sisters.

When she was two and a half years old, Diane started nursery school. She was thrilled. The teacher was kind, and she had long hair that made her very beautiful. She didn't have the goddess's problem, she liked girls as much as she liked boys and she showed it openly. Diane was such a good little girl that the teacher adored her; when she took her in her arms, Diane felt her long hair caressing her face and went weak with delight.

As a rule it was Mamie who came to pick her up when school was over. The teacher gave her a kiss on both cheeks and said, "See you tomorrow, sweetheart!" Swooning with happiness, the little girl jumped up in her grandmother's arms.

Sometimes it was Maman who came to pick her daughter up. The transfer of power between the two goddesses could prove tricky. The teacher would hurry over to tell Marie all the good things she thought about Diane. She failed to see how the mother pursed her lips and the daughter turned pale.

One day in the car Maman said to Diane, exasperated:

"I cannot stand that woman, I'm going to send you to a different school."

The child had the presence of mind to declare: "At the

cafeteria she wouldn't let me have seconds of the chocolate mousse."

Maman must have revised her opinion, because there was no further talk of changing schools.

In the meanwhile, Nicolas was growing, and following in his sister's footsteps: he was handsome, intelligent, advanced for his age, and charming. Diane cherished her brother and spent hours playing with him: she would pretend she was a horse and gallop around with Nicolas on her back. When she whinnied the little boy laughed.

Olivier told his wife he could never thank her enough for such happiness. The little girl thought that jealousy was not solely a bad thing: without jealousy, how would she have known that her mother loved her father? As for the rest, she tried to understand it. There must be a reason for this jealousy: otherwise, why would a goddess gifted with every quality stoop to such an attitude?

Diane loved her mother so much that by the age of four she grasped her mother's disappointment, how she felt that life had unjustly fallen short of her expectations. Even if she had made progress in life, she was still no more than an accountant at her husband's pharmacy, not a Queen, and while her husband might be the most attentive, infatuated spouse imaginable, he was still not a King. The little girl's love for her mother was so great that it could even encompass what her own birth must have meant to Marie: resignation, the end of her faith in some kind of ideal. Nicolas's birth had not sealed her fate in any way, and that too was why Maman showed him her affection.

When she saw the goddess kissing the little boy, leaving her out, Diane managed to move beyond her pain and remember that some day she would become Queen, not out of personal ambition, but in order to hand the crown to her mother and console her for everything in her life that seemed so constricting.

Every night, she remembered that sublime embrace she had known when Maman still had Nicolas in her tummy: her mother's tight embrace, her words of love, the voice she had used. The memory transfixed her with happiness. She suffered from the fact that Marie had never behaved that way toward her again, yet she had built such a myth around the brief spell of hugs and kisses that she knew she could find there all the fervor and energy she would need to ascend the throne.

Nicolas, too, had started nursery school, and his first teacher was delighted to find so much of his beloved older sister in the boy. Diane appreciated this dynastic phenomenon, and supposed, rightfully, that it would endure.

Maman was pregnant yet again.

Nicolas said that she had a melon in her belly.

Diane explained to him what it meant.

"How do you know?"

"Because I remember when you were in there."

In secret Diane prayed the new baby would be a boy. It would be better for everyone, starting with the baby. Maman, too, would be happier: she was radiant when Nicolas was born.

As they could not exclude the possibility of a girl, Diane prepared a strategy: she would smother the poor little thing with affection to console her for her mother's coldness. Because it might be too much to hope that the unfortunate child would display her older sister's fortitude from the outset. Moreover, the newcomer would have to put up with the mother's marked preference for her older brother: how could she bear such an injustice?

All children pray, although they do not necessarily know to whom. They have a vague instinct of something that is, if not holy, at least transcendent. Diane's parents and grandparents did not believe in God. They went to mass so as not to disrupt the social order. The little girl asked Mamie to go with her to church. The grandmother found it normal, and asked no questions.

Diane tried to listen to the priest's prayer and soon realized that she did not understand what he was talking about. As this did not matter to her, she joined her hands and prayed to God that her mommy's third child would be a boy. When Mamie brought Diane home to her father, she said, "Olivier, your daughter was praying fervently—I've never seen anything like it."

Papa burst out laughing. The little girl was ashamed.

For the evening meal Olivier prepared soft-boiled eggs for Marie. She made a face.

"But when you were pregnant with Diane you wanted them all the time," he said.

"Yes. Now, just the sight of them makes me nauseous."

The little girl was delighted: wasn't this the proof that the baby was not a girl?

"Okay. Would anyone like these eggs?" asked the father.

"I'll have them," said Diane.

She loved the experience of it: you thought you were eating a hard-boiled egg and then, no, the yolk was runny, and the color was infinitely warmer and more beautiful. "When Maman had me in her tummy, she ate them all the time," she mused to herself, fascinated. Did that explain why this particular meal had such an effect on her? She trembled with pleasure and emotion.

"It's my favorite meal," she declared.

Her imagination combined these two new things. When she went to mass again with Mamie, the church seemed to her like some giant soft-boiled egg whose yolk was God, running inside her if she prayed very hard; she felt as if the magical color were spreading all through her.

Similarly, when she ate the soft-boiled eggs her father was in the habit of making for her, she would eat the white first, saving the delicate yolk for last as she gazed admiringly at it in her plate: this was God, since it didn't spread. She asked for a spoon, so as not to destroy the miracle, which she placed whole in her mouth.

In June the teacher told Mamie that Diane was ready to start primary school: "She won't be the only five-and-a-half-year-old child to start first grade. She's very intelligent and very well-behaved."

Grandfather joined them, very excited, and told them that the baby had just been born and they had to hurry to the hospital.

"Is it a boy or a girl?" asked Nicolas.

"A girl."

Her heart sank. She was worried for her unfortunate little sister, and, as the car pulled away from their house, she prayed for her, not without also reflecting on the uselessness of her prayers, which had not stopped God from picking the wrong sex for the third child.

Nothing turned out as expected. Maman was not rosy with happiness, she was ecstatic: like the Virgin holding up Jesus, she showed them a round-faced baby and said, "Meet Célia."

Unlike her older siblings, who had always been featherweights, Célia was chubby, like babies in commercials.

"What a fine little round baby!" said Mamie in greeting.

"Isn't she?" answered Marie, holding the newborn to her breast.

Diane could see there was something wrong. When Nicolas was born, Maman was happy and loved her baby; this time, Maman was delirious with joy, overflowing with love for Célia. She kissed her as if she were going to eat her. Over and over, possessed, she said things like *How I love you, my sweet sweet baby.*

It was obscene.

Nicolas ran to his mother and asked if he could kiss his little sister.

"Yes, darling, but be careful, don't hurt her, she's fragile."

Papa and the grandparents looked on, adoringly. No one noticed that Diane kept well to one side, stiff, incapable of moving even an eyelid. Hypnotized by the scene, she composed a silent speech to this woman to whom she would have given everything:

Maman, I've accepted everything, I've always been on your side, I've gone along with you even when you were blatantly unfair, I put up with your jealousy because I understood that you had expected more from life, I endured it in silence when you begrudged me other people's compliments and made me pay for them, I tolerated the fact you lavished tenderness on my brother and never gave me so much as a crumb, but now, what you are doing here before me is evil. Just once, you did show me your love, and I knew there was nothing better on earth. I thought that you couldn't demonstrate your love because I was a girl. But now, there before my eyes, this creature on whom you are showering the deepest love you have ever shown—this creature is a girl. The explanation I have given for the workings of the universe is crumbling. And I understand that, quite simply, you hardly love me at all, you love me so little that it doesn't even occur to you to hide your mad passion for this baby in any way. The truth is, Maman, that if there is one virtue you are lacking, it is tact.

In that moment Diane stopped being a child. She did not become an adolescent or an adult: she was five years old. She was transformed into a disenchanted creature who was obsessed with not foundering in the abyss that this situation had created inside her.

Maman, I have tried to understand your jealousy, and the only thanks I get is this abyss that you have opened before me, into which you have fallen, and it even looks like you'd have me fall into it, too. But you won't get away with it, Maman, I refuse to become like you, and I can tell you, without even having fallen in there, just sensing the call of that abyss, it hurts so badly I could scream, it is like a void closing around me. Maman, I understand your suffering but what I don't understand is why you care so little for me, in fact you are not trying to share your hurt with me, you simply don't care if I suffer, you don't see it, it's the least of your worries, and that's the worst thing of all.

She acted as if everything were fine. She had to. Diane kissed Célia as warmly as she could, and no one noticed the death of her childhood.

That summer was hell. There was no more school to distract her. Every day meant renewed awareness of this abject situation—Maman coming down to breakfast cooing and chirping with Célia, whom she almost never put down, and Diane struggling every moment against the pull of the abyss inside her: she mustn't hate this baby, this debauchery of maternal love wasn't her fault, even if she couldn't help but find the baby's attitude somewhat accommodating—who could guarantee that in her place she wouldn't have done the same, she mustn't hate Maman, who yielded to these excesses without the slightest display of modesty toward those around her—yet again her cruel lack of tact.

Diane had shown that she could understand a great number of inhuman things. That her mother preferred her brother: she had accepted this with exceptional generosity of spirit. Most children wouldn't tolerate not coming first in their mother's affections, especially when they're the eldest. But Marie had scorned Diane's nobility so immoderately that the little girl could never forgive her.

By mid-August, when she couldn't take it anymore, she asked if Mamie could look after her.

"What's the matter, sweetheart?" asked her grandmother.

The little girl couldn't answer. Her grandmother looked her in the eye and saw there was something wrong. Because she loved her, she did not ask for an explanation. But the nonchalance with which Marie agreed to entrust Mamie with her eldest child gave her a fairly good idea.

Before long Nicolas, too, realized something was wrong. His mother went on loving him, but there could be no comparison with the transports of love she experienced with Célia. When he saw that Diane was seeking grandmotherly asylum, he told his elder sister that he would stay at home, "to stop Maman from eating Célia as if she were some coconut cake."

This was no mere image: Marie's excessive love for Célia evoked the swooning of certain thirteenth-century saints when swallowing the communion host. It was holy gluttony.

Olivier was not unduly worried that his eldest child wanted to go and stay with her grandparents: he knew she adored them, and she would be home on weekends. He shared Marie's passion for Célia: even if he did not feel it quite so intensely, he did think the newcomer was particularly delectable. When his wife held the infant in her arms, he embraced the indivisible duo, and melted.

He was a good father in that he loved his three children deeply and showed them his affection. But his love for his wife blinded him to her faults and to the hurt she was inflicting on Diane. He always managed to justify their quirks in a way that was reasonable and acceptable.

When his mother asked him why his eldest child spent the week with his in-laws, he replied that it made things easier for Marie, who had so much to do, what with the baby, and that Diane had always had a special relationship with his wife's parents. He added that she was a big girl now and was already showing a need for autonomy.

When his father expressed his surprise that Marie did not seem to be in any hurry to get back to her work at the pharmacy, whereas, after Nicolas's birth she had started up again quite soon, Olivier answered:

"She doesn't want any more children. She knows this is her last chance to stay home and play mommy, and she wants to devote all her time to it."

Play mommy: this ridiculous expression was a gross oversimplification of his wife's behavior. Only fear of what others might say coerced her into putting the baby into its cradle at night, otherwise she would have kept it in her own bed. In the morning she awoke already in a state of obsession over her latest offspring: she ran to the little bed and seized hold of her beloved with a tender moan (my chocolate croissant, my little warm brioche), and began to eat her up with kisses. This consuming love never stopped. When Marie drank her coffee, she would nibble her daughter's cheek between two sips, the way others take a puff on their cigarette. During the day, no matter what she was doing, she always had Célia by her side, most often in the baby sling she had received when Diane was born and that she had never used. Now she adored the baby harness because it allowed her to feel the love of her life constantly pressed against her belly.

Oddly enough, she did not breastfeed her. She had never thought of doing so for either Diane or Nicolas. For Célia, it did cross her mind. In 1977, however, it seemed to her that to do so would have tarnished her image as a modern mother, and the baby herself would have blushed at such a prehistoric mode of feeding.

The baby sling was a fantastic invention. If she had not been afraid of looking like a frazzled mother, she would have returned to work at the pharmacy with the child on her belly. It was extremely important to her to seem to have everything under control, to look the accomplished woman.

Be that as it may, Célia was a sort of redemption for her. With her child in her arms, she at last stopped seeing herself from the outside. However extravagant her maternal tenderness might seem, it allowed her to view things from another angle than purely that of the envy they might arouse.

Marie only went back to work at the pharmacy two and a half years later, once Célia started nursery school. For all that her two older siblings were ideal pupils, well-behaved and thoughtful, the youngest turned out to be unbearable, accustomed as she was to having everything her way. The teacher mentioned this to Marie, who gave a shrug.

One day when Célia was sobbing and screaming and rolling on the floor in the classroom, it occurred to the teacher to send for Diane. The little girl immediately grasped the nature of the problem and followed her former teacher. She found her little sister behaving like a wild beast and walked resolutely up to her.

"Right, that's enough, now," she said. "You're not a baby anymore, Célia. You can't behave like that at school."

The little girl immediately obeyed. Henceforth, every time she threw a tantrum, they would send for Diane's help.

Célia revered her big sister: eight years old, so serious and beautiful. Diane felt an irascible affection toward the spoiled child, which she hid behind the kindly authority of the wise older sibling.

She often talked about it with Nicolas:

"Since you're with her during the week, don't hesitate to act the older brother around her. It's not Célia's fault if Maman is crazy about her."

"Not her fault—I don't know about that."

"She's never known anything else."

The fact remained that when Diane spent the weekend at home she found it difficult to maintain her self-control. When she saw Célia in her mother's arms, crushed with love, she remembered the embrace of the woman who had once been her goddess, and she felt the abyss of despair open inside her once again.

At lunch on Sundays, she waited impatiently for her aunt to arrive, for this meant salutary distraction. And on Sunday evenings, when she once again occupied her quarters at her grandparents', she let out a sigh of relief: the ordeal was over. Safe and sound, she could reconnect with ordinary life.

She was an excellent pupil, and both her teachers and schoolmates valued her presence. She was a good classmate and had neither enemies nor immoderate friendships. A well-adjusted little girl, who hid her wound well.

Even if it was not premeditated, it somehow suited her, not to have a best friend. She had observed the way the mob behaved: telling secrets, going to slumber parties, and sometimes even going so far as to cry on the chosen one's shoulder. Diane viewed these practices all the more dimly in that she could not allow herself to indulge in them. How could she have confessed her secret to anyone?

Her grandfather occasionally tried to bring up the subject with her:

"You know, your mother was a temperamental child. She didn't have good grades at school, and got demerits on her report card for her unruly behavior. At home she could sulk for hours and you never knew why. How can you expect her to see herself in you, when you are first in the class, you smile all the time, and everyone likes you?"

Diane didn't answer. Could there be an explanation for her pain? Her mother didn't realize she was being cruel. She seemed convinced she was an excellent mother. Marie shared a trait of ordinary people, when she came out with nonsense like, "You know me, I always want to be fair," or, "My love for my children is more important than anything." The little girl watched her closely when she voiced this sort of statement: her mother actually believed what she was saying.

Deep down, Diane thought people were crazy. For mysterious reasons, her grandparents had been spared this collective dementia. She had eventually concluded that even her father and brother were infected by it: her father did not see anything pathological in Marie's maternal attitude, and her brother merely put up with it. As for everyone else, to be sure, it was none of their business, but how could anyone fail to marvel at the sight of this woman who, except during the school day, went absolutely everywhere with Célia? Olivier went no further than a half-hearted attempt to dissuade his wife from continually carrying a four-year-old child around in her arms:

"Honey, it's bad for your back."

In fact, Diane was sorry her mother took his comment into account. If she had gone on making a public display of carrying around a child who was clearly too old for it, people might have begun to notice just how pathological her behavior was.

As if she'd been reading Diane's thoughts, Mamie said, "What can we do? Your mother isn't deranged enough for us to intervene. She's not a good mother with you, or with Célia. But the law can't do anything about it."

All the more so as Nicolas was there to attest to her mental health: with him, Marie behaved like a normal mother, affectionate and reasonable. How could anyone qualify as toxic a family environment that had begotten such a well-balanced boy?

On Friday evenings, when Diane went back to her family, her father threw his arms around her and cried, "My princess." Her brother kissed her and showed her his new treasures: tennis shoes, comic books, Duplo sets. His mother merely muttered, "Oh, so you're here," and went on her way, accompanied by her satellite, Célia. Célia venerated her sister but didn't dare show it in front of her mother.

When Diane questioned Nicolas, all he did was shrug and say, "Maman is nuts around Célia, that's all. Everything else is fine."

"What does she say about me when I'm not here?"

"She never talks about you."

When Célia turned six Olivier decreed that she couldn't go on sleeping in the same room as her parents. They put her in Diane's room, where there were now two beds.

Diane went into a mood when they confronted her with the fait accompli. The first night with Célia was trying. For a start, she had to put up with the endless farewell between mother and daughter: "No, my darling, I'm not abandoning you. It's just at night, it won't be for long. You're a big girl now, you can't go on sleeping with Maman and Papa. Your big sister will watch over you." All of which was repeated a dozen times, with tears on the part of both child and mother.

Olivier eventually came to get his wife, asserting it was time to let the little girls get to sleep. Need one point out that Diane was not entitled to any sort of goodnight from her mother?

No sooner were they alone than Célia rushed over to her sister's bed.

"Maman said you have to watch over me."

"Leave me alone, I'm sleeping."

"I'll scream, and Maman will scold you."

"Go right ahead."

Overawed by such firm behavior, the likes of which she had never seen, the little sister put her arms around the big one.

"I love you, Diane."

"What's gotten into you?"

"Why aren't you here during the week? I love you so much. I feel better when you're here."

"Yeah, really."

"No, it's true. Maman loves me too much, she never leaves me alone."

"You love it, and you always ask for more."

"I don't know what to do."

Diane could sense the truth of her words and she turned to her sister.

"You have to tell her it's not okay."

"But I love Maman."

"Of course you do. And that is precisely why you have to tell her, because you love her. You have to tell her she has to leave you alone, that all her kisses are making you sick, and she's keeping you from growing up."

"You tell her."

"If I tell her, she won't understand. It has to come from you."

"When should I tell her?"

"When you're alone with her. And now go back to your bed."

"Please, can't I sleep with you?"

"Okay. Just tonight, then."

The little sister snuggled up against her big sister. Diane couldn't help but feel a certain tenderness. Célia was adorable—it was undeniable. She fell asleep with her arms around her.

The next morning, when their mother called Célia for her bath, Diane suspected her sister might take this opportunity to speak to her, so she hid behind the door.

"Maman, you have to leave me alone," she heard.

"What are you saying, sweetie?" asked Marie, with alarm in her voice.

"You have to leave me alone. You're making me sick with all your kisses."

"Don't you like my kisses?"

"Yes, but there're too many."

"Forgive me, my darling," replied the mother, on the verge of tears.

Diane held her breath. So it worked! And then she heard:

"Diane told me to tell you."

"Ah! Now I understand. Your sister is jealous, that's all."

"Why is she jealous?"

"Because I don't give her as many kisses as I give you, sweetie."

"Why don't you give her as many kisses as you give me?"

"Because she's cold. And she always has been. Do my kisses really bother you?"

"No, Maman, I love them."

The big sister, who by then had heard enough, went away, distraught. She sat down on her bed and thought: Jealous, me? Whatever next! And if I behave coldly towards you, Maman, it's because you've forced me to be that way.

At the age of eleven Diane felt her world collapsing around her. She'd managed to survive thus far because she thought her mother was blind to her suffering. Now she had discovered that, in her mother's version of events, she was at fault for her mother's lack of tenderness. There was something almost comical about the accusation of jealousy. How could she go on living, stifled as she was by this feeling of insane injustice?

She went through the rest of that Saturday like a zombie. That night, Célia joined her in her bed. Diane didn't move.

"I talked to Maman."

"I know, I heard."

"Eavesdropping is naughty."

"You're right, go and tattle on me to Maman."

"She said that—"

"I know what she said. You're an idiot, Célia, to have told her I had anything to do with it. You lied. You're the one who came and complained to me. I will never trust you again."

"What does that mean, trust?"

"It something you certainly don't inspire in me. Go back to your bed."

Célia did as she was told, sniffling and sobbing. Diane knew she was being harsh: what could a six-year-old child possibly understand about all this business? But she was in such pain that her sister's fate was a matter of complete indifference to her.

A few days later, on her way home from school, Diane had to make her way around a construction site, and she stepped out into the street. She saw a truck heading straight for her. Hypnotized by the speeding vehicle, she did not get out of the way. He braked too late and she was knocked down. The terrified driver called for help. He told the ambulance driver how oddly the little girl had behaved; fortunately, she was not seriously hurt.

It was Olivier who took the call from the hospital. He rushed over there and took his daughter in his arms.

"My darling, what happened?"

Diane told him she had been afraid and hadn't had time to run back to the sidewalk.

"Promise me you'll be more careful from now on."

A doctor had been present during their meeting. When Olivier asked if he could take his daughter home, the doctor replied that he would rather keep her under observation until the following day. Once her father was gone, the doctor went to look at his young patient. He sensed she was smart enough that he could speak to her candidly.

"Do you want to live, or do you want to die?" he asked gravely.

Stunned, Diane opened her eyes wide. She sensed the

question required an honest answer and she thought about it. After a minute she said, "I want to live."

The doctor weighed her statement and eventually said, "I believe you. You can go home tomorrow."

Diane spent the night in her hospital room thinking about his words. The doctor had asked her one question. The one she had not dared ask herself. Just by listening to her short conversation with her father, and observing her, he had understood. With one question he had changed her fate, not only because she had decided to live, but also because at last she had a goal: to practice this man's profession.

She would become a doctor. She would observe people and listen to them carefully, she would probe their bodies and their souls. In the course of conversations as casual as the one she'd had with the doctor the night before, she would pinpoint what was wrong and save human lives. The lightning speed of her diagnoses would be astonishing.

To find a goal for oneself at the age of eleven changes everything. What did her lost childhood matter? What she wanted now was to become an adult so she could attain the sublime status of M.D. Life would lead to something important, it would no longer be a matter of putting up with absurd torment, because even suffering could serve to explore the suffering of her patients. What she had to do now was grow up.

In high school Diane saw her classmates give themselves over to the first throes of love. From one day to the next, boys and girls who had spent years playing ball together began to look at each other differently. At first, there were ties of evangelical simplicity. Then came the experience of breaking up, which inaugurated the era of complexity. What broke their hearts was not the end of the love story, but the speed with which an ex fell in love again. Some of them, out of pure diplomacy, played close to the vest. The situation became Machiavellian. You know longer knew where you stood.

That was how gossip got started. Who was dating who? And yet you were sure you saw Thingummy kiss Thingamajig. Yes, but that was yesterday. In the meantime a lot of water had flowed under the bridge.

Diane wondered whether her mother had not been right, in the end, to qualify her as cold. She looked down on all her friends' little games. When girlfriends shared their secrets with her, she said, "You know it's all just an act!" And her girlfriends would reply, "You'll see, when it happens to you!"

As she was the prettiest girl in the class, she had her admirers. She turned down every single request point blank. She devoted most of her time to studying. She was constantly to be seen in the library, consulting biology books of discouraging proportions.

Her grandparents voiced their concern:

"You're so serious. You should be out having fun with your friends."

"I don't like having fun. It's boring."

"You'll dry up, all this time you spend with your nose in books."

"I don't feel like I'm drying up."

And indeed, as she turned fourteen, every morning her beauty was more striking. She did not suffer from acne or adolescent puffiness; she grew in slenderness and wisdom. People who did not know her thought she must practice ballet, for her every gesture, however insignificant, seemed choreographed. She was always very well-groomed, and wore her black hair up in a chignon. In an era when girls thought it was the height of cool to come to class wearing ripped jeans and a flannel shirt, she wore the severe outfit of a city-dwelling classical ballerina.

"You are a borderline pain in the butt," said Karine, who considered herself Diane's most lucid friend.

"Why borderline?" was Diane's enlightening response.

Disconcerted, the other adolescents respected her, but spoke to her less and less. But no one would ever have dared make fun of her, even in private: there was something about her that inspired fear and discouraged meanness.

Her mother was still the only individual who did not fall under the spell. One sign of progress was that Diane didn't even try to please her anymore. When they saw each other on the weekend they simply greeted each other politely. It was not that the young woman had reached the level of indifference she aspired to, and which would have curtailed her suffering, or that Marie had stopped feeling a rush of jealousy at every flattering remark her eldest daughter received; it was simply that the nature of their bond was that of two spectators, and by no account that of two mutually engaged participants.

Diane's love for her grandparents continued to grow, all the more so as they were beginning to decline. Her grandmother coughed from morning to night, and her grandfather's cholesterol levels were alarming. She was sorry she was not already a doctor, to be able to look after them. She dreaded their death and feared she might not have her diploma by the time the tragedy occurred.

The lycée changed her life. For the first time, Diane saw new faces. She noticed a blonde girl with a lovely, haughty face. Karine whispered, "Look at that preppy girl!" She was wearing a white blouse and gray flannel slacks, as if she had to be in uniform. When the time came for introductions, the stranger spoke in a deep voice that Diane found incredibly classy:

"Élisabeth Second."

Peals of laughter greeted her words. The teacher sighed:

"Your real name, Mademoiselle."

"That is my real name. My parents are Monsieur and Madame Second. And, as they are not without a sense of humor, they called me Élisabeth."

"Is that why you take yourself for the queen of England?" someone shouted.

"Well done, you're only the 355th person to point that out to me," she said with a smile.

Diane felt an unfamiliar sensation: her soul expanded with enthusiasm and admiration. She hated being fourteen and a half years old, because she could no longer simply march up to Élisabeth and say, "Let's be friends, okay?" She had to brave rejection and put in long periods of effort. Every time she asked her a question, the blonde girl answered with a monosyllable.

"Why bother," said Karine, "we don't belong to her world. What do you like about that idiot, anyway? Are you in love?"

"Yeah, really," sighed Diane, rolling her eyes.

Élisabeth had come from a different *collège*, one that was much more upscale and where her mother was a math teacher. Her father was first violin at the Opéra. She did indeed belong to another world, and did not try to hide it.

"Doesn't it bother you to hang out with hicks like us?" a boy in the class asked, head held high.

"No more than it bothers you to be in the company of royalty like me," she replied.

Diane was flabbergasted by her replies. Indeed, how dare she hope for the friendship of someone so exceptionally witty and audacious? The vague affection she felt for Karine was nothing like the fervor that drew her to Élisabeth. She knew it wasn't love, because it didn't hurt in the same way it did with her mother. The pique she felt, that Élisabeth might not like her, merely made her want to fight to win her over.

Karine, who was green with jealousy, told her the place was already occupied:

"Her best friend is the daughter of the orchestra conductor at the Opéra. You haven't got a chance."

"What's her name?"

"Véra," she replied, as if to underline the crushing superiority of Diane's rival.

As they left school that day, Diane saw Élisabeth throw her arms around a chubby dull blonde and cry, "Véra!" She decided all was not lost.

She pulled out all the stops. At every break she went to sit next to Élisabeth. One day she told her, deadly earnest, "You know, the Chernobyl cloud didn't just stop at the border."

"Why are you telling me this?"

"Our life expectancy is bound to be reduced because of the radiation. Let's be friends."

"I don't see the connection."

"You always seem so bored at this lycée. If your life expectancy has been reduced, it's a pity to waste the time you have. With me you won't be bored anymore."

Élisabeth burst out laughing. They became inseparable. Diane dared to share her secret. Élisabeth listened in silence and sighed. Finally she said, "Is that why you live with your grandparents?"

"Yes."

As there was no longer any imposition of silence, Diane accepted Élisabeth's invitation to visit. As their daughter was an only child, Monsieur and Madame Second adopted her new best friend: "You will be her sister," they said. The adolescents talked all night long. Diane was tactful, and refrained from asking about Vera; they never saw her again.

Mamie was very glad to learn of this brand-new friendship.

"At last you're behaving like a girl your age! I can die with my mind at ease, now."

"That's not funny, not one bit," said Diane, furious.

And indeed, it wasn't funny: it was prophetic. The next day, the grandparents' car was hit by a truck: the driver had fallen asleep at the wheel. They died instantly. Diane was at the lycée when she heard the news. She lost consciousness.

When she came to, she was at the hospital. The doctor, whom she hadn't seen since she was eleven, was at her side.

"You've been here for a week. You had a temperature of nearly 106 and convulsions. I've never seen someone react so violently to a death."

"My grandparents meant everything to me."

"For the funeral, we couldn't wait for you to regain consciousness. It's better that way: it would have been unbearable for you."

Diane wept, sobbing uncontrollably.

"I didn't even have a chance to say goodbye!"

"You'll go and commune with them on their grave. There's something else, young lady. I remember you. I had a chance to speak about you with your family and your best friend. You won't be going back to your parents' to live. Your friend's parents are prepared to take you in."

"How did my mother and father take it?"

"Your father seemed a bit hurt. Your mother simply said that she wasn't surprised and that it would be better if you didn't visit on weekends anymore. Rest assured, your friend has told me everything."

Diane opened her eyes wide.

"Do you think my mother hates me?"

"No. Your mother was surely jealous of the bond you had with her parents. She loved them very much. It would be better, both for you and for her, not to have anything more to do with her for a while."

"So I'm losing not only my grandparents but also my parents, my brother, and my sister, all at the same time."

"You'll see your brother at the lycée. And you'll see your parents. Someday, your relationship with your mother will no longer be toxic. I think that for the time being it would be dangerous for you to spend too much time in her company."

"And my sister?"

"I am aware of the overinvestment she is receiving. There are no laws against pampering a child to such a degree, but in a way she is more deserving of pity than you are."

Monsieur and Madame Second welcomed Diane with affection: she was their daughter's sister, and thus their child. Diane had her own room, next to Élisabeth's.

A new life began. At least three nights a week the girls went to the Opéra to attend concerts.

"Why did you never go before you met me?" asked Diane.

"It felt like an obligation. Now that I've met you it's a pleasure."

The lycée was rife with gossip. Their classmates called them dykes. The interested parties shrugged it off. Diane lost some of her prestige, Élisabeth found hers greatly enhanced.

Monsieur Second persuaded his new daughter to take up the violin. While he was an excellent artist, he proved a poor professor; as for Diane, she displayed more zeal than talent. The rare occasions when she managed to make her instrument produce a sound that contained some emotion, she burst into convulsive sobs. The experiment came to a sudden end.

Now and then she could see the beauty of her present life, the harmony of her time with the Second family, and she could appreciate the distance she had taken from her former travails, only to relapse all the more grievously when she ran into her brother at the lycée, or when her father, who clearly failed to grasp the situation, came to wait for her after class and gave her a long hug that seemed filled with pain.

The years went by and she continued to mourn her grandparents. One day when she wanted to go and meditate on their grave, she was shocked to find her mother there, in tears. She slipped away again without her mother noticing her, but the pain of seeing her was so sharp that she could measure the extent of the damage in her soul.

Only study was free of danger. She immersed herself in it. She passed her *baccalauréat* exams with flying colors and enrolled in the city's highly reputable medical school. As she did not want to be beholden to anyone, she found a temporary job over the summer.

Élisabeth bemoaned the fact she would not be going on vacation with her and her parents the way she had the previous summers. She herself had enrolled in law school, with the aim of becoming an attorney.

The start of classes meant the pace of Diane's life became frenetic. Medical school provided access to better paid student jobs, but it all required massive amounts of energy.

Élisabeth complained that her friend never had any time to spend with her, so she turned to more ordinary affairs of the heart, consistent with her age. She managed to drag Diane along to the odd party, but Diane was bored stiff.

"Your friend is so pretty, but she always looks so pissed off," people told Élisabeth.

"She likes to put on airs," she replied.

Others liked those airs. Admirers came in droves: the game was to see who could get her to smile. No one could.

Élisabeth got more seriously involved with a certain Hugues. She neglected Diane, who was filled with sorrow; out of pique, Diane took up with someone by the name of Hubert, but she was not in love with him. As for Hubert, he was madly in love with this aloof, mysterious girl. When they made love it was as if she were not there. This was painful to him, and made him yearn for her all the more.

"I'm not in love with you," she told him one morning as she left for class.

"It will come," he replied, darkly.

It didn't come. After three years, she found the courage to leave him.

"How could you stay for so long with a man you didn't love?" asked Élisabeth.

"It was either him or someone else . . . " was all Diane said.

"You're such a strange bird. Then why did you break up?"

"Because I cannot help but hope for something better."

Élisabeth found her answer reassuring, even though she did not see how her friend, who was working twelve hours a day, would ever find the time to meet the man of her dreams.

In her seventh year of medical school, as she was about to become an intern, Diane decided to specialize in cardiology. One of the assistant professors, a Madame Aubusson, made a great impression on her.

Extraordinarily eloquent, Madame Aubusson was the epitome of rigor and intelligence. Whereas other professors irritated Diane with the vagueness or boastfulness of their lectures, Madame Aubusson was precise and serious, like no one else.

The young woman soon realized that she was attending Madame Aubusson's lectures with more than just mere interest: what she felt as she listened to her brilliant presentations was of the nature of passion.

Madame Aubusson was an assistant professor most likely in her early forties, a little red-headed woman with a handsome, imposing face. She dressed her small body in austere pants suits, which enhanced the brilliance of her hair. When she spoke, her eyes sparkled, and she became the most attractive person imaginable.

Diane got into the habit of waiting for her at the end of the lecture to share her enthusiasm. Flattered by the compliments of this exceptionally lovely young person, the instructor behaved toward her in a friendly manner, and one evening she suggested they go for a drink.

"Call me Olivia," she said, after they had spoken for a few minutes.

"I don't know if I can call a professor by her first name."

"Maybe not in class. But here, you can. Besides, I'm not a full professor."

"Why not?"

"It's a long and rather boring story. In the end, perhaps it's better that way. Look at Michaud, Salmon, Pouchard: they're all full professors. Do you think I want to look like them?"

Diane laughed.

"They're useless!" she said.

"I wouldn't go so far as to call them useless," said Olivia. "Let's just say that their elevated status has gone to their heads, and it hasn't improved them."

She then began imitating the solemn, hollow delivery of Yves Pouchard, professor of vascular surgery, and Diane wept with laughter.

"Yes, indeed, that is what happens when you become obsessed with status," concluded Olivia. "The thing that I'm obsessed with, is training good practitioners and teaching them rigor. I am dismayed by the vague approach of some of those who teach our specialty. If we educated our nuclear physicists the way we educate our cardiologists, we would have Chernobyl every day. After all, it seems to me that the heart deserves as much serious attention as radioactivity, if not more, don't you think?"

Diane wasn't listening anymore. She hadn't thought about Chernobyl since the day she'd said the name with the intention of winning Élisabeth's friendship. Wasn't it strange that at the dawn of a new, important friendship in her life, there had once again been mention of the disaster?

"You're not very interested in what I'm saying," said Olivia. "And you, why did you chose cardiology?"

"It happened in two stages. At the age of eleven I decided I would study medicine, because I met an extraordinary doctor. As for cardiology, I warn you: my motives might seem completely idiotic."

"Go ahead."

"I was impressed by a quote from the work of Alfred de Musset: *Strike your heart, that is where genius lies.*"

Madame Aubusson was transfixed.

"I did warn you," said Diane, very embarrassed.

"Not at all. I think that's wonderful. I had never heard that quote, or come across such an astonishing reason to study cardiology. *Strike your heart, that is where genius lies.* Alfred de Musset, you said?"

"Yes."

"What a guy! What a revelation! Do you know, he was right? It's an organ like no other. I understand why the ancients believed that was where thoughts were located, and the soul, and all that sort of thing. I've been observing the heart for over twenty years, and it seems more mysterious and inspired than ever."

"I was afraid you would make fun of me."

"You must be joking! For once one of my students has some culture! I wish I had some."

"I don't have that much culture, you know. But I've always liked reading."

"You'll show me. How wonderful: I've only just met you and you've already enriched my life."

The evening continued in this vein. When Diane got home, she was in an altered state: she had never felt so enthusiastic about someone. The fact that this superior woman was interested in her, and even went so far as to let her believe she might enrich her life, was extraordinary. How generous she must be, to suggest such a thing!

The next day, the assistant professor rang her.

"Are you having lunch at the hospital cafeteria?"

"Like you are, I believe."

"What would you say to having lunch with me at the local brasserie?"

Diane joyfully accepted. At the brasserie, Olivia ordered a salad which she hardly touched. Diane did not dare order anything more substantial and she was not sorry: she was in such an emotional state she found it hard to swallow.

Madame Aubusson confided in her quite openly. She told her how difficult it was to be a woman in this milieu. "I don't know which are more macho: the male students or the male faculty."

"Do you think that has anything to do with the fact you're not a full professor?"

"It's bound to. Particularly as I had a child, ten years ago. They never forgave me for it. But if I hadn't had a child, I'd have been judged even more harshly. Even when you teach at university you still can't get away from their provincial mentality."

"Have you always lived here?"

"Yes. I confess I'm very attached to our city. Yves Pouchard, now, dreams of only one thing: moving to Paris. Can you see him at the Descartes campus, reading those notes of his he always seems to have just discovered, so that he makes one blunder after another? One day during a lecture instead of blood tests he said bloody tests!"

"Seriously!"

Olivia had dozens of similar anecdotes to tell. Their lunches became a routine. When the two women arrived at the brasserie they did not even need to order: they were immediately served their two salads and a big bottle of mineral water. It was a bit light for a lunch, in Diane's opinion, but for nothing on earth would she have done things differently.

Her bond with the assistant professor gave meaning to her life. She wanted both to be like her, and to be on her team. Everything she had been reproached with since childhood—her seriousness, her rigor, what her mother called her coldness—was, at last, appreciated. Diane was jubilant whenever Olivia displayed these same virtues.

There were times when she heard students in the auditorium murmuring "Aubusson doesn't seem very friendly," or "I'll bet she gives you a hard time." Diane forced herself to keep quiet. If she had dared speak out, she would have said, "Olivia Aubusson is a major heart specialist. She isn't here to be friendly. When you reach that level, you don't need to be friendly. And anyway, you'd be surprised to find out how funny she can be."

Their complicity had not gone unnoticed, and it was cause for a few predictably sarcastic remarks, among both students and interns.

"It's because you're very beautiful," said Olivia with a laugh.

"You're not bad yourself."

"Finally someone who's noticed!"

"I can't be the only one."

"Who else?"

"I don't know. Your husband?"

"Stanislas is a mathematician. He doesn't say things like that."

Diane was dying to ask her more about her life. But the feeling that it would be indiscreet prevented her. Everything about Olivia seemed phenomenal to her.

Onc day as she was leaving the university she saw a woman waiting for her. Initially she did not recognize her.

"Diane, is that you? You've become so beautiful!" said the woman.

"Maman!" said Diane, petrified.

She had not seen her mother for ten years. She'd had neither the time nor the inclination. Sometimes she would meet up with her father, always at his request, and he merely lamented their estrangement, without ever calling his wife's behavior into question. What had happened to her? She seemed broken, ageless, her features ravaged.

"May I speak to you?" asked her mother.

They went to a café.

"What's going on?"

"Célia has left."

"What do you mean?"

Marie burst into tears and took a letter from her bag.

"Your sister has had a child. Did you know that?"

"I think I heard something," Diane replied, with a shrug.

"It was last year. She wouldn't tell me who the father was. I wouldn't be surprised if she doesn't even know. Since turning eighteen Célia has done nothing but go out, and she drinks a lot. Rumor has it that she has had a lot of affairs, with older men."

"Spare me the gossip, okay?"

"In short, she had a daughter, Suzanne. She left a week ago without telling me where she was going, and she left her little girl behind, with me."

Still crying, Marie handed Diane the letter she was holding tremulously in her hands.

Maman,

I can sense I am beginning to make the same mistakes with Suzanne that you made with me. I love her too much, I can't help holding her in my arms all the time and covering her with kisses. I don't want my daughter to become a spineless wreck like me, who's only good for sleeping with any man who comes along. Besides, I'm twenty years old and I want my life to begin.

So I'm going far away, and I won't tell you where. I'm leaving Suzanne with you. I can see that you love her, without going stark raving mad over her the way you did with me. Maybe with my daughter, at last you'll be the person you never were with your own children: a good mother.

Célia

Diane sat there flabbergasted for a long moment, not knowing what to say, her head bent over the letter.

"It's terrific, what she's done," she finally managed to say.

"You think so?" said Marie through her tears. "And here I was wanting to ask you to go and look for her."

"Are you crazy? I would never do such a thing. For a start, because I approve of what she's done. And then because even if I didn't approve, she is an adult."

"How can you approve of this?"

"She doesn't want to repeat your mistakes. And that's a damn good reason to leave. She doesn't want to smother Suzanne beneath the mountain of kisses and cuddles you inflicted on her all through her childhood and adolescence."

"It was because I loved her, where's the harm in that?"

"You'll have to accept that it is harmful, because she has complained about it. She complained to me when she was little. I told her to talk to you about it. She tried, but you manipulated her to convince her that it all came from me."

"That's not true."

"Maman, I was behind the door in the bathroom, I heard everything."

Diane looked at her mother's stunned face and saw that she had not been lying: she had forgotten.

"So I was a bad mother?"

"Not with Nicolas. He is fine. I often run into him on campus."

"And you too seem fine."

"No, I'm not fine. I am cold, remember?"

"Yes. You always have been."

"No. I wasn't when I was little. I forced myself to be cold in order to accept the way you were."

"I never mistreated you."

"Maman, I left home when I was fifteen."

"Yes. I never understood why."

"And yet you told the whole town that I couldn't get over the death of my grandparents. Did it never occur to you that I left because of you?"

"No. It was because of me?"

Again Diane could tell that her mother was being sincere. At university and at the hospital she had often observed people's incredible ability to forget: they forgot what didn't suit them, or rather, they forgot when it suited them to forget—in other words, very often. Now she could sense the intensity of her mother's pain, and the sincerity of her forgetting.

"You do know that amnesia is not an excuse, Maman?"

"An excuse for what?" said Marie, who didn't even realize she had forgotten.

Diane was tempted to tell her everything. What stopped her was her fear of going too far. She didn't know whether this too far included the risk of killing her mother, but she did know that no act and no words would bring her relief. On the contrary, instead of setting her free, a confession would drive her deeper, perhaps forever, into the hell of that childhood she had had such difficulty leaving behind.

Could Marie have behaved differently? Diane thought not. Her mother lacked the wisdom; it was impossible for her to take stock. What would be the point of reproaching someone who was incapable of self-analysis, especially with so many years to make up for?

The woman who was looking at her with pained curiosity seemed innocent. What absolved her was neither the passage of time, nor her forgetting; it was her demon. Diane recalled how she herself had nearly fallen into the abyss, when she had seen her mother showering Célia with such exuberant love, while deliberately depriving Diane of it. Marie lived in that abyss. The fact she had fallen into it because of some absurd stupidity in no way detracted from the tragedy of her fate. What she had inflicted on her eldest daughter was merely the expression of a warped narcissism of which she had no inkling.

"Are you still jealous, Maman?"

"What are you talking about?"

So her mother was that oblivious. Having said that, if she did not realize she had been jealous, perhaps she did not know whether she had been cured of it. How could she find out?

"Is Célia as beautiful as you were? I haven't seen her for ten years."

"Oh, yes," said Marie. "She is such a lovely young woman! My pride and joy! And yet, I have to say that you are even more beautiful than she is," she added, and Diane did not see a single bitter crease at her lips. "Why don't you come back home? You're only twenty-five, we could try to make up for all the lost time."

She is still every bit as stupid, Diane thought, and sighed. Obviously she would love for me to come and fill in, now that Célia has gotten out of it.

"It's too late, Maman," Diane said simply.

"Too late for what?"

"You know I'm an intern, now. I spend my life at the hospital."

"Apparently you are frequently seen with a woman my age. A professor."

"There you go, gossiping again."

"Who is she?"

"She's an assistant professor in cardiology. Her name is Olivia Aubusson."

"Olivia? How funny. That's the name I had chosen for you."

"Really?"

"Yes. Your father objected."

"I have to go," said Diane, who had heard enough. "Be a good mother to Suzanne, Maman."

"Of course I will," replied Marie, as if it were self-evident. "Goodbye, my daughter."

How sorry Diane was to be on duty that night! She needed to talk to someone. If only she could have gone to see Élisabeth. But, she would never get to sleep that night, so, she thought, she may as well work.

She stayed for hours at the side of an old lady who was allergic to solitude.

Thoughts whirling, tumbling, racing: what her mother had said became so muddled that insignificant words now seemed to contain a dangerous hidden meaning. She was incapable of determining which was more hurtful: the present suffering of this woman who had been a goddess to her, or the negation of her childhood hell. Diane did not belong to that category of people who see their tormentors' torture as a form of expiation. Even if she approved of what Célia had done, she thought it was terrible that she had had to run away and abandon her child in order to keep herself from doing harm. As for Marie's offer to take her back into the fold, she found it downright offensive, a dreadful irony of fate.

Was she crazy to think she had detected sarcasm in her mother's allusion to the fact that Olivia and she were the same age? How could they even be compared? Marie had reached the age of the vanquished, Olivia that of the conquerors. Finally, Marie's revelation regarding the name she had almost given her made her sick to her stomach.

In the middle of the night she felt an urge to tell Olivia everything that had been said. An hour later, she swore to herself she would do no such thing: her experience with this exceptional woman was completely unlike those kinds of friendships where secrets are shared—not that she didn't trust her, but because she would have blushed to confess to such weakness. Who was the author who said that every life was reduced to a miserable little pile of secrets? It was out of the question, she could not share her pile of secrets with Olivia. She wanted to rise to her level, not invite her friend to wallow with her in the mud of her past.

In the end, she would have been happier had this conversation with her mother never taken place. *Home is where it hurts*: the pain she was feeling made her realize she had reconnected with her childhood home.

At six in the morning she went off duty. Classes began at eight, she wouldn't have time to get any sleep. She sat through her lectures like a zombie, then joined Olivia for lunch.

"You look like death warmed over!" said Olivia.

"I was on duty last night."

"But you don't usually look like that the next day."

Diane could sense she was about to give way. To stop herself, she changed tack completely.

"Olivia, I've been thinking: you ought to apply for your *habilitation*[1]."

"What's got into you?"

"I've been thinking about it for a long time."

"And this is why you look like a corpse?"

"You always joke about it. In fact, you're laughing so you won't cry. It's so unfair that you don't have your *habilitation*."

"I don't care."

[1] Roughly the French equivalent of tenure for university professors.

"If you really didn't care, you wouldn't talk about it so much."

"I only talk about it to bad-mouth the ones who do have it."

"Precisely. But you deserve to be a full professor."

"Stop right there, you don't know what you're getting into. To apply for the *habilitation*, you have to have published a dozen articles. I would be incapable of publishing a single one."

"But it's not as if you lack subject matter, or the talent to write them."

"The journals that matter for the *habilitation* are all American. You have to submit your articles in English, electronically. Two obstacles I cannot possibly surmount."

"I've always been very good at computers and at English. We can write your articles together."

Flabbergasted, Olivia stopped eating, her fork raised.

"You don't know what you're saying. Even if you weren't completing a cardiology internship, this represents an impossible amount of work. You couldn't do it all at the same time."

"I'll bet you I could."

"And why would you do it?"

"Because it makes me sick that you're not a full professor. None of our professors deserve to be, apart from you. It's an imposture."

"If I decide to go through with this, those same imposters will be my judges."

"Is it worth a try, though?"

"I never made fun of them in public. I showed some regard for their susceptibilities."

"Well then, it's decided."

"Diane, it will take at least two years of back-breaking work."

"All the more reason not to waste any time. Let's get started right away."

"This means that for two years, you won't see anyone but me."

"We get along well. Finish your salad, Olivia, we have our work cut out for us."

Diane felt she had been rescued. She could think about something else besides her mother. As for the prospect of intensive collaboration with this wonderful woman, it filled her with enthusiasm.

In 1997, almost no one had a laptop. In Olivia's office at the university there was a big desktop computer.

"I have no idea how to use it," Olivia confessed.

Diane set two chairs in front of the IBM. Over the two years that followed, the two friends spent all their free time on those chairs. They often stayed there until three or four o'clock in the morning. On Sundays, they brought picnics.

"Who is looking after your daughter?" asked Diane.

"Stanislas is an excellent father. He drives her to school, goes home to work, and is always back there when school gets out. And do you have anyone missing you?"

"No," said Diane, who thought the question had been deftly put.

She was lying. A few days earlier, Élisabeth had grilled her:

"Are you sexually attracted to Aubusson?"

Diane gave her best friend the look Caesar gave Brutus before uttering his final, historic words.

"I wouldn't be shocked, you know," said Élisabeth.

"Nor would I. I'm not shocked. But it's not true."

"What a pity. I would have preferred it if you had been."

"That's quite something!"

"If you desired that woman, I would understand your attitude. But now it completely baffles me."

"Writing these articles with her is truly fascinating."

"So fascinating you can do nothing else? So fascinating you've stopped sleeping?"

"Exactly."

"How much do you weigh now? Ninety pounds?"

"Leave me alone."

"Are cardiologists required to be that thin?"

"The majority of heart conditions stem from overeating and obesity. I prefer to set a good example."

"But you look like a skeleton!"

As it happened, Diane agreed with her. But whenever Olivia saw butter, cheese, or meat, she reacted like a believer in the presence of the devil. All she ate was raw vegetables with a little dry bread.

The first time one of her articles was published, Diane opened a bottle of wine. The older woman looked at her warily.

"It's good for your arteries!" Diane protested.

"Then just a drop."

Despite the austerity, Diane loved collaborating with her. They were able to draw diagrams on the computer that delighted Olivia with their precision. When she saw them reproduced in the journals, she was jubilant.

"Our rigor has won over the Americans!"

Diane was proud of her use of the word "our." And so proud to be supporting such a brilliant woman! What did it matter that she only got three hours sleep a night and never took any vacation? As for her academic results, they had never been better.

Six months before the date set for her *habilitation* defense, Olivia offered her a position as a junior lecturer.

"I'm nowhere near good enough."

"Of course you are. You'll be top-notch."

Three months later, Diane gave her first class. It was a success. "I'm not yet twenty-seven and I'm already teaching at university! Thank you, Olivia," she thought, impressed.

Nicolas invited her to his wedding. She wrote him a very kind letter, apologizing for not being able to attend. "It's a combination of circumstances," she explained. "I'll make up for it later on, as soon as I have more time." Offended, Nicolas did not reply. Diane was hurt, but what was she to do? She had her classes to prepare, her dissertation to write, her shifts to cover and above all, she had to coach Olivia for her imminent *habilitation* defense.

Her father called to express his indignation:

"Your own brother's wedding, you could at least take the time off to attend!"

Diane found it difficult to stay calm. This man who had never bothered to find out why his daughter had left home at the age of fifteen: he was offended, in the name of the family, by her refusal to attend some high-society do.

"Papa," she replied, "try to understand: I have just started teaching at the university, I'm working on my dissertation—"

Her father interrupted, brightly: his daughter was teaching at the university! Such a prodigy had every right.

“Congratulations, sweetheart,” he stammered, and hung up. Diane figured that within the half hour he’d have gone around informing the entire town, inflating his own ego. Far from feeling proud, she was angry.

It was a good thing the *habilitation* process was nearly over! It enabled her to move on to other things. The event itself was quite entertaining. Olivia introduced Diane as her research assistant, and this gave Diane permission to attend the session. It was in no way a forgone conclusion: Olivia had to convince a jury made up of professors who were infinitely less brilliant than she was, without alienating them for all that. She did not hesitate to resort to the customary formulas of flattery: "Owing to the expertise which Professor Pouchard has so kindly imparted to me," or "As Professor Salmon has pointed out in his brilliant article," and so on. Olivia had to demonstrate the coherence of her twelve recent American publications, and this she did, superlatively.

For Diane, this was a successful conclusion. Her friend was awe-inspiring: her eloquence, intelligence, and skill. She thought back over these two years of intense work, their complicity, their moments of despair, the difficulties they had overcome together. To have played a leading role in such a meaningful accession seemed to her to be the most significant thing she had ever done.

At the end of her presentation Olivia went to sit with Diane and the jury retired to deliberate.

"You were wonderful," said Diane. "Bravo!"

"Really?" murmured Olivia, in a trance.

After an agonizing wait, the jury returned. Yves Pouchard proclaimed that Madame Aubusson, with the congratulations of the jury, would henceforth be granted the title of full professor. Olivia crushed Diane's hand before going to shake each juror's.

Once they had left the auditorium Olivia told Diane she would never forget to whom she owed her title.

"The custom is for the newly appointed professor to host a little party. We'll have it the day after tomorrow in the room where the proceedings were held. You'll be able to meet my husband at last—and I'll finally be able to see him again!"

"Can I help you organize it?"

"I think you've helped me enough as it is, Diane. You have your own dissertation to write."

Forty-eight hours without Olivia seemed very strange, after having spent most of the past two years in her company. She was glad to see her friend again on the evening of the party.

"Diane, allow me to introduce Stanislas, my husband."

He was a good-looking man in his fifties, slim and elegant.

"I will let you get acquainted," said Olivia, going off to greet the other guests.

Talking to Stanislas turned out to be a laborious task. He hardly listened to her, and when he did, it was worse. Agitated, he inquired, "Why are you asking me this?" when she had not questioned him at all. And if she did ask him something, he didn't answer. Finally she realized it would be better to say nothing. Silence had an immediate calming effect, and his features relaxed into a pleasant expression. Diane then excused herself, and went off to speak with others. It wasn't easy, no doubt because she was twenty years younger than the majority of the guests, and they all seemed to wonder why she had been invited to the party.

The high point of the evening was Olivia's speech. She stepped up to the podium, visibly moved.

"At the age of fifteen, while reading Alfred de Musset, I came upon these famous words of his: '*Strike your heart, that is where genius lies.*' As adolescents we have such moments of lightning intensity, and I knew at once that I would devote my future to the study of the human heart . . . "

Diane, stunned, did not hear another word.

Olivia's peroration was met with thunderous applause. Yves Pouchard proposed a toast. No one noticed that the young woman had left the room.

The following day, Diane wondered why the incident had upset her so. Alfred de Musset belonged to everyone. After two years of uninterrupted collaboration, it was normal that Olivia had ended up confusing their memories. She swore to give it no further thought.

She met her friend for lunch as usual.

"It went well, yesterday," she said politely.

"It did."

Olivia cheerfully filled her in on countless details. Diane was relieved Olivia had not noticed her early departure.

"What did you think of Stanislas?"

"Ah. What can I say?"

The older woman burst out laughing.

"Forgive me, I should have warned you. His specialization in mathematics is topology."

"What's that?"

"To be honest, I've never understood a thing. But it's a well-known fact that it makes people odd. The only thing to do is not speak to him; then everything is fine."

"So you don't speak to each other?"

"My parents didn't speak to each other, either. I once pointed this out to my mother, and she said, 'Sweetie, we've been married for thirty years. What would you have us say to each other?' I just put this into practice a bit earlier."

Diane would have liked to ask a number of other questions. But she refrained, for fear of seeming indiscreet.

A few days later Olivia informed her that she would be having lunch the following day at the mess hall, with the professors. The mess hall was the name they gave a section at the university restaurant reserved for prominent people.

"At last you'll be able to find out if they have their own special food," joked Diane.

Two days later she went to the brasserie. Olivia did not show up. Nor on the day after that. Diane realized this was her friend's vague way of telling her they wouldn't be having lunch together anymore. She couldn't help thinking that the professorship had gone straight to Olivia's head.

She ran into Olivia in the corridor and greeted her coldly.

"Well, Diane, what's going on?"

"You're asking me?"

"Oh, I'm sorry, I should have realized. Come have lunch at the mess hall with us!"

"When you were an assistant professor you said you weren't allowed into the mess hall. And I'm not even an assistant professor."

"I'm sure that Yves and Roger won't take offence."

"All the more reason not to come, given the fact that for years you kept telling me how much you despised them."

"Shush, someone might hear you."

These last words were too much for Diane and she walked away.

A few days later she found a note in her mailbox:

"Sorry about the misunderstanding. Come for dinner at my place at eight o'clock tonight, nothing fancy."

Diane had tears in her eyes. She'd dreamt for so long of this moment, and at last Olivia was inviting her to her home! How could she ever have doubted her friendship?

Stanislas opened the door. She recalled his modus operandi so she merely said good evening. Without a word he led her into a tastefully furnished living room, then withdrew, leaving her alone. She sat for a long time gazing at this place she had only imagined for so long, and which now turned out to be perfectly ordinary.

"What, Diane, you're here? You should have called me," said Olivia on entering the room.

"I didn't want to interrupt you."

They talked about this and that. Diane was glad to see they had lost none of their closeness. She fell once again under her friend's spell, the sheer force of her personality.

"I'll go get the dinner ready," said Olivia, getting to her feet. "And please don't expect anything special: cooking is not my thing."

Diane went with her into the kitchen and smiled when she saw Olivia had put together raw vegetables and a salad.

"I should have known!" she said.

"Naughty girl, since you're making fun of me, your punishment will be to go and set the table."

While Diane was setting out the plates, she noticed a pair of furtive eyes spying on her. It must be Olivia's daughter. She realized she didn't even know her name.

"Is there someone there?" she murmured very softly.

A little girl stepped timidly forward: she was so small

and thin that she looked only eight or nine years old, but Diane calculated that she must be twelve. The child hardly dared look at her.

"Good evening. What's your name?"

No answer. Olivia came in and said brusquely, "Well, Mariel, has the cat got your tongue?"

The little girl immediately ran out.

"She's so sweet!" exclaimed Diane.

"And very sociable, as you can see," said Olivia.

"She'll outgrow it."

"You think so? Were you like that at the age of twelve?"

"We all grow up at our own pace."

"Grow up? I think that's hardly the word for it."

Uneasy, Diane changed the subject and went into the kitchen to slice the radishes. Five minutes later, she heard an abnormally shrill voice say, "Maman, you have to sign my report card."

Olivia grabbed the report card, quickly scanned the results, gave a sigh, then signed without voicing any comment. Mariel ran out again.

"Is something wrong?" asked Diane.

"Just the usual," said Olivia indifferently.

"May I go see her?"

"If you want."

Diane ventured down the corridor, knocked on a first door, didn't get an answer, opened it and came upon Stanislas, lying on his bed, eyes open, staring at the ceiling. She quickly closed the door again and tried another one. Mariel was sitting on the floor, curled up on herself.

"May I see your report card?"

Terrified, the child said nothing. Diane gently took the pages from her and leafed through them. "Mariel

Aubusson, sixth grade." The little girl was already one year behind. As for her marks, they were alarming. Her teacher or teachers had not dared write any comments, her level was that low.

Her father is a researcher in mathematics, her mother is a professor of cardiology at the university, thought Diane, looking desperately for something positive to say. In the end she saw that in gymnastics the child had progressed from -3 to -1.

"Good girl! You're doing well in gymnastics," she cried, with forced enthusiasm.

Mariel looked up, stunned. Her smile was so disarming that Diane took her by the shoulders and kissed her.

On her way back into the living room, she saw a medal on a bookshelf and was intrigued. Olivia noticed her curiosity and said proudly, "That's the Fields metal. Stanislas was awarded it when he was thirty-nine."

When his wife called him, the laureate, winner of the world's highest distinction in mathematics, sat down at his place, chose his salad leaves one by one, then gazed guardedly at them in his plate. He eventually chewed them in silence. Mariel was no more talkative, nibbling timorously. In the meanwhile, the lady of the house, charming, made conversation, not the least bit offended by their silence. Diane would have enjoyed listening to her had it not been so obvious that the little girl was unhappy.

After dinner, as Stanislas was leaving the room, his wife called out, "Don't work too late, darling."

When she saw that Diane was giving her a puzzled look, Olivia added, "Did you see him lying on his bed staring at the ceiling with his eyes wide open? That's how he does his research in topology. He gets up for four minutes a day to write down his thoughts on a piece of paper. Impressive, isn't it?"

She shone with pride when she talked about her husband.

Diane had brought a box of chocolates. Olivia opened it to have with the coffee. Mariel looked at her mother for permission to take one.

"Help yourself, sweetie," said Olivia.

Was it because of the "sweetie" or the chocolate? The little girl's face lit up with pleasure. She sighed with delight. Diane smiled and suggested she have another one.

"It's out of the question," Olivia intervened. "They're fattening."

"Mariel is as thin as an rail!" protested Diane.

"And she has to stay that way."

Her tone was so harsh that the little girl ran out of the room.

Diane was speechless. Her host misread her and came out with a slew of platitudes: "It's never too late to adopt a healthy lifestyle," or "Excessive consumption of milk chocolate has played a significant role in the rise of cardiovascular disease," and she failed to notice how uneasy Diane was.

Diane found a pretext to leave without further ado. Olivia must have realized she was in a no-win situation, socially, because she piled one entreaty upon another ("What? You're not leaving already? I've been waiting so long for this moment . . . " and so on). Diane cut her short, adding that she had to run but that she could come again the following evening.

"That's a good idea," exclaimed her host, but her tone was neutral.

"I'll come at around six if that's not inconvenient."

Sitting at the wheel of her car, Diane figured she was imagining things. How could there be any similarity between herself as a child and that poor traumatized kid? Above all, how could the oh-so-brilliant Olivia Aubusson resemble her mother in any way? She refrained from digging any deeper.

It became a ritual: every other day, Diane came at six to help Mariel with her homework. In the beginning it was alarming: it turned out the girl knew how to read and write and that was it. Diane carefully avoided asking awkward questions such as, "Didn't your mother or father ever explain to you that . . . " so that the little girl would not realize she was suffering from a grave parental deficiency.

As for Olivia, she never missed an opportunity to pretend to be angry with someone while in fact blaming someone else:

"Diane, don't you think it's dreadful, the way they make mothers feel guilty nowadays? Have you noticed that every pretext is valid to make them feel ashamed they don't look after their children properly? But never a word about fathers."

"You're right, it's intolerable, the fact they don't target fathers as well when apportioning blame. Unless, of course, the fathers are borderline autistic."

"Stanislas is actually amazing, you know. He's always on time to take Mariel to school and pick her up afterwards. It breaks my heart when I see all those children hanging around outside the school waiting for their parents."

"Stanislas is indeed a paragon of precision when it comes to doing his share of the chores."

"Your devotion is touching, Diane, but don't waste your precious time. Mariel will never be a genius, you know."

"I'm just trying to help her get through the year. She's making a lot of progress."

"And what about your dissertation? And your studies?"

"I'm spending less time on your daughter than I did on you, when you were preparing your *habilitation*."

"But that must have been a bit more enriching for you, I would think."

"There's no comparison. But I get along very well with Mariel."

"Such children are endearing, it's a well-known fact."

How is this possible? thought Diane when she heard remarks of this nature. To put it mildly, she viewed Olivia in a very different light now. The only thing that mattered to her was her reputation. Her CV was impressive: a brilliant career, a remarkable husband. As long as you did not try to talk to him, Stanislas was the ideal spouse, and she even had a child, so no one could reproach her for having "sacrificed her womanhood." The very expression raised Diane's hackles. How could someone as intelligent as Olivia have given birth to a child solely for that reason? Diane knew that Mariel had not been an accident: Olivia had told her she'd had trouble getting pregnant.

She's your friend. Don't judge her she told herself, over and over. An inner voice then immediately queried: Is she your friend? To convince herself that she was, Diane had to think back to the time before the *habilitation*. Alas, what was left of that magical complicity they had once had?

The same Olivia who had once made her laugh hysterically when she mocked the mannerisms of the academic establishment had now adopted every one of them. She no longer spoke formally with the professors, but said *tu* to them and was on a first-name basis, and seemed surprised if anyone did not understand who she was referring to ("What do you mean, which Gérard? Michaud, of course!"). She had enrolled in their sports club, and never missed an opportunity to meet up with them. Deep down, even if it irritated her, it also suited her to have Diane act as babysitter, as she put it: it freed her to get on with her social obligations, leaving Stanislas and Mariel in the young woman's care.

Looking after Stanislas was easy: as long as dinner was served at eight o'clock on the dot, he showed no signs of discontent; in other words, he showed nothing. Diane was filled with retrospective indignation at the thought that for over two years the little girl's sole companion had been this silent, brooding father.

Olivia's attitude has changed, that's true, but less than my attitude towards her, she admonished herself. How could she feel the same friendship toward Mariel's mother as before?

I'm not being objective, I'm seeing her through my own childhood memories, she thought. It was clear that the little girl's unhappiness was reactivating her own. And I had my grandparents, my father, and my brother. During all these years she's had no one to give her either attention or affection. It didn't take a genius to infer that the little girl had no friends her age and never had.

Mariel and Diane grew very fond of each other. The moment Diane arrived at the house, the little girl threw her arms around her. Diane did not merely help her with her homework. When she saw that her hair was dirty she suggested she should wash it more often. The little girl replied she didn't know how and that it was her mother who washed it, "sometimes."

Diane washed Mariel's hair above the bathtub. Then she took hold of the hair dryer and told Mariel to lean forward: while she was drying her hair, she could feel that the little girl was pressing her forehead against her belly and she shivered, because she recalled positioning herself in exactly the same way with her mother when she used to have her hair dried as a child. And she remembered the emotion she had felt at the time, on discovering this potential for contact with her goddess.

But I was six years old when I did that. When you're twelve, it's a bit late.

She taught Mariel how to wash her hair.

"I have to speak to you," said Olivia one evening, once Mariel was in bed.

"I'm listening."

"I would like to spend more time on research. Since the *habilitation*, I've been tending to rest on my laurels. That won't do. But as it happens, I have a lot of ideas."

"Good for you!"

"That's where you come in. Could you take over my lectures every other time?"

"I'm no professor, I wouldn't know how."

"Oh go on. Of course you would! You are an exceptionally intelligent young woman. You can do whatever you set out to do."

Flattered, Diane registered the compliment:

"Thank you. But it will demand a lot of time."

"I've thought about it. Your time won't be wasted. It will be extremely useful for your dissertation, for your studies, and it goes without saying, for obtaining your title as assistant professor."

"I'm nowhere near ready for that!"

"We'll get there."

Diane did not fail to pick up on the "we," and wondered how she ought to interpret it.

"Obviously," continued Olivia, "you'll have less time to look after Mariel."

She had her answer. All the same, she pretended she hadn't understood:

"I'll always have time for Mariel."

"Of course. It's so kind of you," said Olivia.

Diane recognized that bitter line at the corner of her lips. She remembered her grandmother's words: to impose its reign, jealousy needs no motive. That had been true for her mother. And now it was so true for Olivia! So, you could be a university professor, not to mention a charming, accomplished and beautiful woman, and still be jealous of the attention a former admirer paid to your sickly, traumatized daughter.

Because this was not nostalgia for a fading friendship. If that had been the case, Olivia would have resorted to a sentimental register. The worst of it is that it would have worked, thought Diane. It's a good thing she doesn't see me as anything more than simply ambitious. Let's pretend to go along with that.

Diane was more overworked than ever. Between her own classes and Olivia's, her dissertation, her ongoing studies, her nights on duty, and the hours she devoted to Mariel, she got an average of two hours' sleep a night. "I don't know how I'm coping," she thought. Her fatigue was so intense that if she had the choice between eating and sleeping, she never hesitated: sleep had become her holy grail. At this rate she was losing more weight than ever.

"Watch out," said Olivia, "you're losing your looks."

In the light of such ambiguous solicitude, Diane played the role her former friend had assigned her: the woman who wants it all.

Her engine was running on an explosive mixture of love and hatred. The love was for the little girl, whose progress was encouraging: Mariel was now obtaining near-satisfactory results in every subject. Diane never failed to congratulate her with hugs and kisses. The little girl's radiant face was reward enough for her efforts.

Olivia was right: Diane was a brilliant stand-in at the lecture podium. Initially disconcerted by this teacher who was scarcely any older than they were, the students, on the whole, were enthusiastic about Professor Aubusson's assistant. At the end of her presentations Diane felt a feverishness she could not explain.

As for hatred, that was more complicated. When she was in Olivia's presence she sometimes wondered, "How do you know when you hate someone?" It was easier to hate her in her absence: she would think of how she sometimes behaved toward Mariel, and she felt an urge to shove the woman's face in a mud puddle. "That must be hatred," was her diagnosis. Apart from these intense moments, what she felt for Olivia was more like fathomless disappointment. "That's a generous thought: it proves I expected great things of her."

Just as she was finishing a tricky passage in her dissertation, someone knocked at the door to her office.

"Come in," said Diane.

It was Élisabeth. She had neglected her for so long that she was astonished to see her there in the flesh.

"You never answer your phone, so here I am."

"Forgive me, I've been working like a madwoman."

"You look like a zombie. Tell me what's going on."

Diane explained her professional situation. Élisabeth frowned.

"I hope she's paying you?"

"Of course she is. With money she's always been above board."

"So there are areas where she is less so?"

"What are you insinuating?"

"Don't you think she's using you?"

"No. She didn't want to become a full professor. I'm the one who persuaded her to apply for her *habilitation*. I had to insist."

"Sure. And now she's so unhappy to be a full professor."

"Of course she's happy. That's natural. You can't criticize her for that."

"I'm not criticizing her. I just think it probably wasn't that difficult to persuade her to apply."

Diane thought she had a point.

"Why are you here, in fact? You didn't come all this way just to check whether I was alive?"

"I came to invite you to my wedding," declared Élisabeth.

"What?"

"Here's a quiz for you: who am I marrying?"

"No idea."

"Your best friend is getting married and you don't even know who the groom is. Bravo."

"I know, I've been distant over these last months, I'm sorry."

"Over these last years, you mean. I warn you, I'm not like your brother: I won't allow you not to come to my wedding."

"Who's the lucky man?"

"I won't tell you. That way you'll have to come. I'll leave you in suspense for now."

"Not my brother, I hope?"

"Are you crazy? In case you'd forgotten, he's already married."

"Maybe he got divorced in the meantime."

"You've broken off with everyone, apparently. Shall I invite Olivia?"

"No. Why?"

"The polite thing is to invite both partners in a couple."

"I already told you, we're not a couple."

"Things may have changed. In any case, if you're not in a couple with her, you're not in a couple with anyone."

"If that's what you wanted to know, all you had to do was ask."

"You've become so prickly! Listen, the wedding is on March 30. If you're not there, I will come and get you. You can't get out of it."

March 30 seemed a long way away. But the months went by incredibly quickly. She worked so hard that time no longer had any pulp. All that remained of each day was its core, and it was not she who was biting away the flesh.

One morning in January she realized she was twenty-eight years old. "And if I was forty-six, what difference would it make?" she thought, apathetically.

At that rate, March 30 was approaching fast. On the fateful day she realized she had nothing to wear. In her wardrobe she found a matching skirt and top. The clothes were so loose on her it was a pitiful sight, but at least they were elegant. I don't care, she thought. What does bother me is that I'm going to waste a few hours when I could be working.

Magnificent in her white tailleur, Élisabeth introduced her husband, a certain Philippe, who seemed likeable enough (at least the suspense was worth it, she thought). Monsieur and Madame Second were delighted to see Diane again; she was surprised to feel so emotional on seeing them. It reminded her of a page in her life she thought she had turned forever.

On her way to get a glass of champagne, she was astonished to see Olivia in the crowd of guests: she had clearly come straight from the hairdresser's and was eagerly joining in the small talk.

Diane hurried over to Élisabeth to ask why she had invited her. Élisabeth replied that she had sent her an invitation as a matter of form, and she was surprised when Olivia immediately accepted.

"I invited her with her husband, and he's here, too. Is that a problem for you?"

"No."

It was all the less of a problem in that Olivia had not noticed her presence. "So this is how she spends her time on research. And this is why I have to assume responsibility for half of her classes," thought Diane. But, she could not help but feel enchanted. Where was the austere woman she had met three years earlier? Olivia's outfit was exquisite, and the slightest thing made her burst out laughing. Men and women alike only had eyes for her. "Where has all her stiffness gone?" wondered Diane.

Alas, she knew the answer. As she was putting on her makeup for the wedding, she had been struck by the dryness of her face. It was worse than thinness. What she had lost was grace, and it was grace she now saw radiating from Olivia.

For a split second she had been pleased to see how beautiful her former friend had become. But all at once she felt her soul split in two and open onto an abyss, and she knew that her entire self would be sucked into it, so powerful was the lure of that bottomless pain.

"There's no way. I cannot capitulate to this degree," she reasoned. She had to look elsewhere, urgently. A bit further along she saw Stanislas, lost in the contemplation of his glass of fruit juice. She thought that Mariel would be alone at home, and Diane had only one desire, to go and be with her, and get away from this masquerade.

Manifestly, this was not the case for Olivia. Not looking at her, Diane inched closer to hear what she was saying:

" . . . your son, yes, I know exactly, Maxime, a very bright young man. It's a pleasure to teach him." Diane had to hold back her laughter, because Olivia never memorized her students' first names. And then, "Yes indeed, I've been teaching at the university for over twenty years. You wouldn't know? How kind of you! To be honest, I work so hard I don't have time to get old!" You bloody hypocrite, snickered Diane. With relief she felt that the abyss in her soul had closed.

"This champagne is exquisite!" she heard. "Is it Deutz? Ah yes, I'd know it anywhere. I always say that the purpose of life is to drink fine champagne." Now it was all Diane could do not to burst out laughing. Olivia avoided champagne like the plague: she was afraid it would make her lose her self-control. Diane could not help but glance at Olivia's glass: it was almost full.

"Can't you look at someone else?" said Élisabeth.

"I asked you not to invite her."

"I'm not sorry I disobeyed you. It has allowed me to assess the gravity of the situation."

"Have you finished judging me?"

"I'm not judging you. I'm concerned. You are drifting into a horrible situation. Believe me, do what you can to stop seeing that woman. Well well, speak of the devil."

Olivia was coming toward them to congratulate the bride, and she pretended to suddenly notice Diane's presence.

"What? So it's you, this lovely coat hanger?"

"Research suits you, you look splendid," Diane replied.

"Yes, it's quite clear that you have had precious help," added Élisabeth.

Sensing that the situation was not in her favor, Olivia

smiled and allowed herself to be lured away by one of the many guests who wanted to speak to her.

"She's so full of herself!" said Élisabeth.

"She wasn't like that when I met her."

"Will you stop making excuses for her? She's revolting! Just look at how she's jabbering on and blowing her own trumpet: you went to so much trouble so she could become a full professor, and now she uses it to prance around in high society. Now I order you to go and stuff yourself with petit fours. It distresses me how thin you are."

"I'm sorry about the other day," said Olivia to Diane, one evening when she had come to take care of Mariel.

"What are you talking about?"

"At your friend's wedding. I was absurdly unpleasant to you. I don't know what came over me."

"I've already forgotten it."

"So much the better. You mean a great deal to me, you know. Which reminds me, I have a suggestion to make."

Here we go, thought Diane, dreading yet more work.

"I would like to use *tu* with you," said Olivia with a smile.

This was so unexpected that Diane opened her eyes wide. She was touched, and eventually agreed.

"Is that all right? Oh, this makes me so happy. It's so much more congenial."

"You'll have to bear with me," Diane implored. "I'll probably get it wrong half the time."

"No problem. We should have begun saying *tu* a long time ago. I thought of it now because I heard Mariel saying *tu* to you."

Diane suddenly felt enraged. I should have known, she thought, how could I have thought this was a sign of friendship, when it was only jealousy toward her daughter?

She went on to bitterly regret this new familiarity. Abandoning the use of *vous* meant that Olivia now left off any last traces of respect she might still have shown her. Formerly she would say: "Excuse me, have you finished correcting the mid-term exams?" Now this was reduced to: "Right, are those corrections done?"

The most notable absentee from the whole experience of saying *tu* was the *tu* herself. Olivia was not even addressing a person anymore.

Diane gathered all her remaining courage to inform Olivia that she could no longer teach half her classes.

"My dissertation defense is in September. I'm nowhere near ready."

Olivia could not see the inconvenience—after all, it was only April.

"I'll help you," she said.

"That won't be necessary."

"I can share with you the tricks I've learned," Olivia insisted.

And why not, after all? thought Diane.

Olivia's devotion astonished her. Instead of going on vacation, she spent all summer with her. She gave her quite clever advice. Nothing fundamental, but it could turn out to be useful.

One week before her defense, Diane ordered Olivia to go spend a few days in the sun.

"You've done enough for me. I'll take care of Stanislas and Mariel."

"Thank you for looking after the children," said Olivia with a laugh.

*

The day before Olivia was due back, Diane tidied up the Aubusson apartment. She happened upon a large manila envelope that had not been sealed, and without thinking she checked the contents. They were the corrected galleys of an article Olivia had written. The article was based on the most personal and brilliant aspects of Diane's dissertation; her name did not appear once in any of the footnotes.

She put the sheets back in the envelope, sat down, and thought.

"I am not going to compromise my future because of this monster. She's a member my thesis defense jury. I'll grit my teeth until tomorrow. Then I'll break off with no explanation. Otherwise I'll end up killing her."

Breaking off with Olivia meant breaking off with Mariel. The prospect grieved her, but that would still be better than killing the girl's mother.

That evening, when she tucked Mariel in, she kissed her more tenderly than usual.

"Sleep well, my darling," she said, closing the door behind her.

She went over her dissertation one last time then went to bed. Astonished by her own coldness, she drifted off.

On D-day, she went to pick Olivia up at the station.

"Shouldn't you be cramming?"

"I know everything by heart. You look great."

The defense began that afternoon. Conscious of the degree of hatred she had attained, Diane exerted more self-control than ever. She didn't need to look at her notes even once. When she began developing the topic on which Olivia had based her article, she turned to her in particular. Olivia did not stop beaming with pride for one moment, as if she were the source of such excellence.

The two other members of the jury asked a few questions. Diane gave brilliant answers then thanked the professors for the "considerable help" they had given her. The jurors withdrew to deliberate and returned before long. Diane was awarded her degree with the congratulations of the jury.

Olivia invited her to come over to celebrate. Diane said she would rather have dinner with her at their brasserie, like in the good old days.

Delighted to see them again, the waiters automatically brought them two salads and a bottle of mineral water. While she ate, Olivia complimented Diane on the quality of her defense.

"I already knew you were good at oral exams, but there, you really impressed me."

You ain't seen nothin' yet, thought Diane, thanking her.

When the last lettuce leaf had been ingested, Diane said she had something to tell her.

"I'm listening," said Olivia.

"I'm leaving the university."

"Pardon?"

"You heard me."

"You can't do this to me."

"It has nothing to do with you. My intention has always been to work with patients, not teach."

"But you're such a divine teacher!"

"Even if that were the case, it would change nothing."

"And you come and tell me this abominable news right after your defense?"

"Why are you so shocked? Would you actually have penalized me if I'd told you before?"

In Olivia's eyes she read, "You're making fun of me! Damn right I would have penalized you!" She pretended she hadn't noticed.

"And how will I manage without you?" said Olivia indignantly.

"It's sweet of you to say that," said Diane, pretending to misconstrue her meaning. "You don't need me."

"Of course I do! Where will I find the time to devote to research!"

"You've made a lot of headway with your research over the last months."

"I see. You've been going through my things!"

"I don't know what you're talking about."

"Stupid fool. That's the way researchers have always

done things! If you're bothered by something so trivial, it means you just don't have a clue."

"What on earth you are talking about?"

"That's it, go on acting all innocent. You'll see what's in store for you: patients. Patients are the dregs of humanity. You'll miss your students, girl."

"I'll miss the professors more than anything."

"Laugh it off, dear, laugh it off. In the university, life is imbued with intelligence. You'll see what it's like, dealing with heart patients: nine times out of ten, the pathology is caused by excess fat, and the treatment means putting the patient on a diet. When you tell them to stop eating butter, they'll look at you as if you were a murderer. When they come back three months later and you're surprised there's been no change, they will tell you a blatant lie: 'Doctor, I don't understand, I followed all your recommendations.' When we opt for cardiology and research, we opt for nobility; when we practice as doctors, all we do is treat pigs."

"I don't mind being a vet," said Diane with a smile.

"How can you forsake your intelligence—someone like you who is allergic to stupidity?"

"It's not only stupidity I'm allergic to."

"Go on then, out with it."

"You already know."

"I know what you blame me for more than anything: you think I'm a bad mother. What right do you have to judge me? We'll see what sort of mother you turn out to be, if, like me, you're unlucky enough to have a kid who's not as smart as you."

"I won't be a mother."

"How do you know?"

"I just do."

"Well, I can see what you mean. When I met you, you were as pretty as a picture. Now what's left of all your splendor? Who'd even look at you, now?"

Staggered by her harsh, treacherous words, Diane stood up and walked out. She heard one last cry of rage:

"Don't ever come to my house again, you're not welcome! You'll never see Mariel again!"

That's the one sad note, she thought.

That night, on going to bed, she knew she wouldn't sleep. She was proud she'd done what she had to do, but for all that, she was deeply unsettled by how angry Olivia had been.

She had always thought that Olivia's contempt stemmed from her dealings with individuals who were worthy of it, such as those influential muck-a-mucks whose failings she had justly railed against before the doors of the academic establishment opened to her and she became their best friend. But now Diane understood that it was in this woman's nature to look down on others. She was a scornful person, she sought out objects of contempt and found them easily: anyone naïve or sickly, even her own daughter. And me too, no doubt, from now on, she thought.

"Be sparing with your contempt, there are many who need it." Olivia did not need to obey Chateaubriand's wonderful precept, because she had contempt to spare. She could dole it out, lavishly, and always have some left over.

The rewards of contempt include the feeling of superiority vis-à-vis its object. Therefore Olivia did not deprive herself of any opportunity to indulge in it. Yet to feel such a need implied that what separated her from those she looked down on was flimsy indeed, as illustrated by her attitude toward the top academics. Did the same apply to her attitude toward those who had weak hearts?

Diane recalled a conversation they'd had over a year earlier, which at the time had seemed unimportant. She had asked the woman, who was still her friend at the time, whether she had a history of heart trouble, given how carefully she watched what she ate.

"No. But I want to stay slim," she replied.

"It doesn't seem to me that you would ever put on weight."

"Before my daughter's birth, I could eat as much as I liked. But now I put on weight with the least little thing."

Diane recalled the bitterness in her voice. Might this be one explanation for her loathing for Mariel?

If only it had been no more than hatred! It now seemed to Diane that contempt was worse than hatred. Hatred is close to love, whereas contempt is completely foreign to it. At least my mother never looked down on me like that, she thought. She trembled at the thought of Mariel's fate.

The morning after that sleepless night Diane saw she had a message in her inbox from Olivia. "To think I'm the one who taught her how to use the internet!" And she was the one, too, who had shown her how to check whether her message had been read. Diane decided not to read this final message. She knew Olivia well enough to be certain that it would make her explode.

"Stupidity lies in wanting to draw conclusions," wrote Flaubert. This was rarely better illustrated than in quarrels, where the imbecile could be identified by their obsession with having the last word.

Inexorably true to form, life went on.

Diane was practicing full time in the cardiology department at the hospital. Her patients adored her: no matter the nature of their problem, she listened to them with so much respect that they were able to change their habits, if she asked them to.

Despite her work load, she had adopted a much healthier lifestyle. She began sleeping again at night, and her appetite came back. And with it, she soon regained her beauty as well.

She decided to get back in touch with her family. Her father was sorry she was no longer teaching at the university, but he was very proud to have a daughter who was a doctor. Her mother, perfect in her role of caregiver to little Suzanne, got into the routine of inviting Diane for lunch every Sunday, along with Nicolas and his wife and children. Brother and sister were effusively happy to be together again.

Every year on her birthday Marie received a postcard from Célia. Judging by the postmarks, she was circumnavigating the globe on foot.

Élisabeth had two sons, Charles and Léopold. Diane was Léopold's godmother, and she was exceedingly fond of the two brothers, who called her Auntie.

Diane had no lack of suitors. She rejected every one, without exception. She never saw Olivia again. Sometimes she got word of her. It was always an unpleasant experience.

Five years later, she heard that Mariel had dropped out of school. This left her with a feeling of great sadness.

And the years went by. Diane became the owner of a pretty house in the nicer part of town. To her immense joy she discovered the art of gardening.

In January 2007, Diane turned thirty-five. A few days later, two policemen came to her door. She gazed at them, astonished.

"Olivia Aubusson was murdered at some point between the evening of January 15th and the morning of January 16th. We'd like to ask you a few questions."

Stunned, Diane let them in. The night of January 15 she had been celebrating her birthday at Élisabeth's place. She had not seen the victim in seven years.

"How was she killed?"

"Twenty stab wounds to the heart."

For a long while she sat there speechless. Then, "Her husband?"

"He is in a state of shock. He lies on the bed and stares at the ceiling."

"Did he see the murderer?"

"No. They had separate rooms. But we ask the questions. Was Olivia Aubusson having an affair?"

"How would I know?"

"You were very close to her."

"Yes, for three years, we were friends."

"What was the nature of your friendship?"

"Professional, mainly. I also looked after her daughter for close to a year."

"Tell us about her daughter."

"Mariel. At the time, she was twelve. Since then, I heard she left the lycée, that's all I know."

"Did she get along well with her mother?"

"I have no idea. Ten years ago, she adored her."

"Outside the victim's residence we found tire traces that were not from her car. Do you know whether Mariel drove?"

"How should I know?"

"We ask the questions. Why did you stop seeing Olivia Aubusson?"

"We had a disagreement."

"Of what nature?"

"Professional. I did not want to go on working with her at the university."

"Why not?"

"It was not my vocation. I wanted to be a doctor, not a teacher. She took it badly, the discussion got heated. Our friendship came to an end."

They questioned her further, obtaining confirmation only of her ignorance of recent matters concerning Olivia Aubusson, then they left, but not before asking her to get in touch with them if any elements of interest came to mind. Before leaving, they took Élisabeth's contact information in order to verify Diane's whereabouts on the night of the murder.

Diane did not need to think long to figure out who the murderer was.

When you kill someone with twenty stab wounds to the heart, it is a crime of passion. She knew for certain who had shown Olivia unrequited love for nearly twenty years.

Was it not infinitely graver than a love affair that ends

badly? A love so deep, so incurable and vital and inconsolable: and Olivia's sole response had been contempt.

The choice for the date of the murder was a signature addressed to her, Diane. To commit the act on the evening of her birthday, the murderer must have loved Diane. Not that the murder was intended to make her happy, but so that she would be in no doubt as to the perpetrator's identity.

In 2007, the murderer would turn twenty. The same age as Célia when she abandoned Suzanne and fled from her mother. The gravity of the punishment would correspond to the gravity of the crime. Marie's crime had been far less serious than Olivia's. Marie had been blind, and mad. Olivia had been coldly, lucidly contemptuous.

Diane recalled that the murderer's birthday was on February 6. All she had to do was wait.

On February 6 Diane stayed home all day. At 23:54 there came a very quiet knock on her door.

"Happy birthday," she said immediately to the girl she let in.

She might be twenty, but Mariel looked sixteen. She was small and thin, and in her huge eyes Diane could read boundless hunger.

She did not ask the girl any questions.

"I have nowhere to go," said Mariel.

"This is your home."

About the Author

Amélie Nothomb was born in Japan to Belgian parents in 1967. She lives in Paris. Since her debut on the French literary scene a little more than a decade ago, she has published a novel a year, every year. Her edgy fiction, unconventional thinking, and public persona have combined to transform her into a worldwide literary sensation. She is the recipient of the French Academy's 1999 Grand Prix for the Novel, the René-Fallet, Alain-Fournier, and Jean-Giono prizes.